# DANCING WITH DEATH

## A STARLIT DESIRES NOVELLA

## GW PROUSE

PROUSE BOOKS

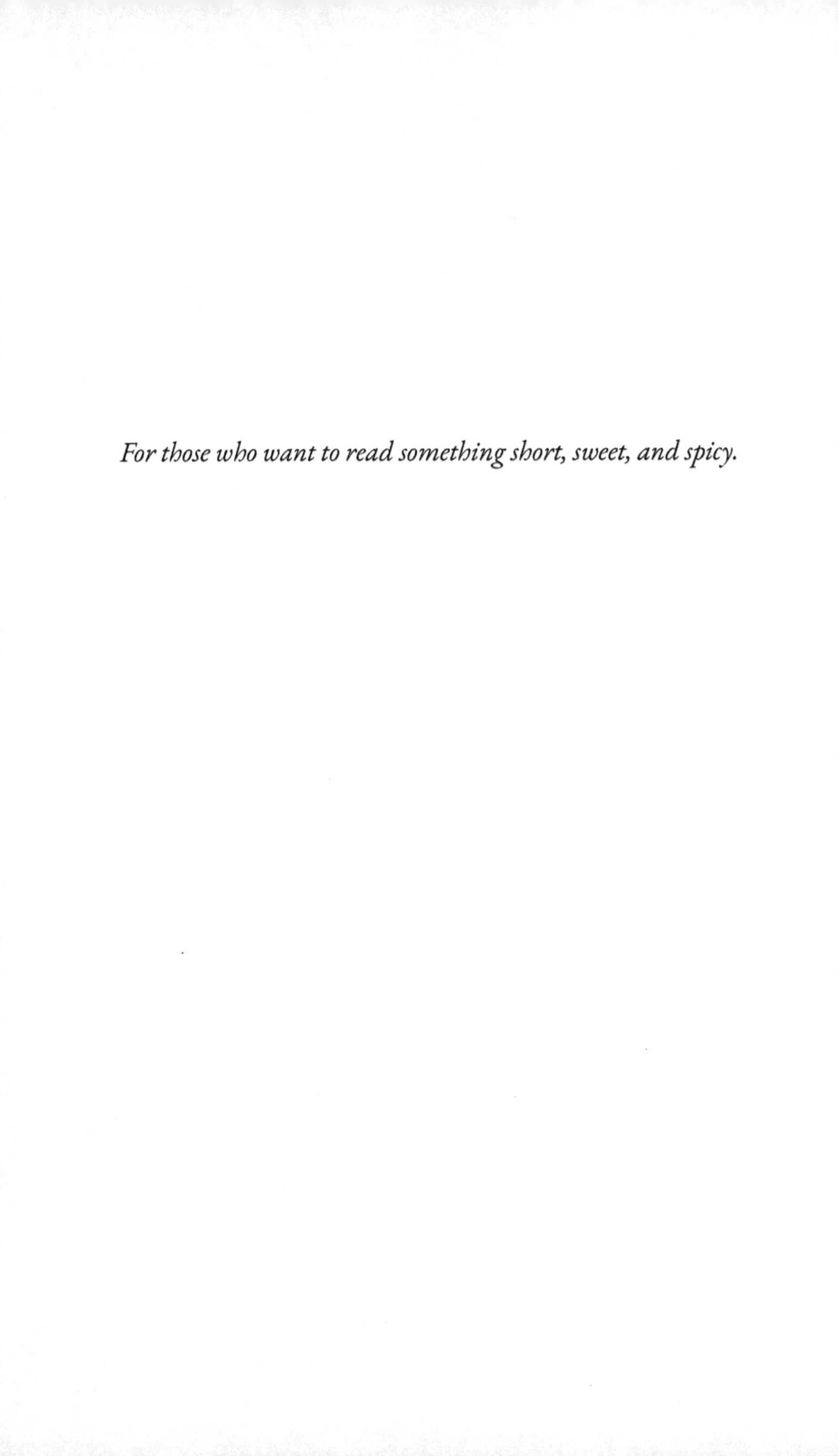

*For those who want to read something short, sweet, and spicy.*

# NOTE TO READERS

This novella should not require you to read its predecessor, *Isle of Waiting* unless you choose to do so. *Dancing with Death* does have more descriptive sexual scenes than the "New Adult rating" *Isle of Waiting* possesses. There is an introduction to characters and a short overview of *Isle of Waiting* included for your perusal.

*Dancing with Death* is a fictional novella with themes of recurring grief, talks of death of a sibling and adult child, graphic sexual encounters, and conversations of individuals falling under the power of immortals (i.e. desire, lust). If you need further clarification, contact the author, but please take care of yourself over reading anything that may be triggering for you.

# CHARACTERS

**Kora:** A mortal who is tied to the Isles of Nekrós by pomegranate seeds that saved her life. Hasn't admitted she's in love with Shade

**Shade:** King of the Dead and ruler over the Isles of Nekrós. In a relationship with Kora

**William:** Kora's deceased twin brother. For more on his story, read Isle of Waiting

**Michael:** Kora's little brother who also visited the Isles of Nekrós when she attempted to save her twin's life

**Captain:** AKA Theileus- King of the Gods. He spent fifty years away from his throne in an attempt to force Shade back to his post

**Helieus:** The King of the Sea who caused havoc and Kora slapped on one instance in Isle of Waiting

**Astrea:** Queen of the Pixies who lives on the Anamoní (The Isle of Waiting)

**The Triad:** the three Gods of Love which includes the trickster, Velos (Desire), Thélo (Lust), and Áxios (True Love)

**Apóle:** the Goddess of Heartbreak

# A SHORT OVERVIEW OF ISLES

In Isle of Waiting, Kora made a deal with Captain (aka Theileus- The King of the Gods) to return his brother, Shade, to his post as ruler over the Isles of Nekrós. In return, he said he will save William, her twin brother's, life. Shade's choice to leave his title fifty years before caused Captain to remove the immortals from the mortal world. Because of this, a famine spread, causing many to suffer, while Captain took over the passage of the souls while attempting to force his brother back to his title.

Up to that point, Shade had thwarted all attempts until a young woman who he'd unknowingly allowed to see him upon the collection of her twin's soul, appeared on the shore of the Isle of Waiting (Anomoní).

Kora did everything she could to find the fruit that would save her brother's life and force Shade back to his title. She uncovers that her presence on the Isle has awoken unexpected powers. As she fights her growing attraction and empathy for Shade and her want to save her brother, Kora finds herself in the midst of a battle between the two immortals that almost takes her life. Shade regains his post, and with the pomegranate fruit, saves her life, also tying her to the Isles.

Due to choices William made, he can't return to the mortal world and she is allowed to say goodbye to him before he crossed to his resting place. Once a month she must return to the Isles, which both she and Shade prefer as they have fallen for each other. For more, read Isles of Waiting...available online wherever books are sold.

# CHAPTER 1

KORA SHIFTED THE SOIL ASIDE, making space for the sprouting seedling she had nurtured on her windowsill during the past month. The vine and leaves of the fasolakia plant hung over the mosaic pot it started in. After transferring it to fresh soil in her garden, she patted the dirt around it before winding the vine around a trellis.

Today marked the end of her first semester at the University of Athens and since she returned home she'd been in her garden. With a glance over her shoulder to be certain no one came from the house, she removed one of her gloves and pressed her fingers into the dirt. Power radiated from her hand, checking the temperature of the soil. She chose a location under the bow of an olive tree slowly healing in the hopes it would keep the soil cool enough for a late crop. Another experiment to see how much control she had. Too cold and the seedling would slowly germinate, and its development would be hindered. Too hot and it would damage the stem and roots. Either way, it would kill the plant.

Kora closed her eyes, feeling for the roots buried within the dirt, stretching them gently so they took hold and settled. A brush against her hand startled open her eyes, and she found one of the vines twined around her fingers.

She gasped, pulling back at the sight of the bean plant now twice the size it had been. "I didn't mean to do that," she whispered, checking her surroundings once again and relaxing after determining she was still alone. There were only two options:

hope her family remained clueless to the advanced growth of her garden or wither the plant and start again.

She didn't like to waste, though, so she chose the former. Her family didn't pay close attention to the strange happenings since she returned from the Isles or chose not to question their replenishing bounty and how it came to be. For the first month after her return, the power that had been unlocked on the Isles of Nekrós had seemed dormant. Plants flourished at her touch and care, but nothing more. Until the day an Attica artichoke had grown out of control. She had attempted to reverse the growth, but her power caused it to wilt and the plant died, taking with it all the progress she had made.

Kora brushed her hands together to remove as much dirt as she could, then leaned back on her heels to survey her work. Oregano and anithos grew, overtaking one of the garden beds to her right. Various species of bees buzzed, disappearing within blossoms of violets and poppies as they collected pollen. To her left was a fig tree and wires that held grape vines. In the far corner was an orange tree that had been given extra attention in the past week. Its branches hung over the fence, shading the walking path that led to town. Kora only trimmed back the branches when necessary, happy for passersby who took the fruit as a snack.

The recently built block wall allowed for more privacy and opportunities to take chances with her experiments and the power that dwelled within her. Prior to its construction, there had been multiple break-ins, even as the famine had started to subside. When her garden began to flourish, those who traveled through the neighborhood into town would look over the previous picket fence with curiosity and jealousy. The people of Athens didn't know if they could trust that the desolation had ended. She understood their skepticism. They didn't have her knowledge about the immortals who had once abandoned them.

The gods had returned. The world was in order again. The weather and climate stabilized, and the seasons were back on track. The plants and animals began to thrive. With her community's eyes turning towards her and her garden's success, she could only show Athens through her actions to trust that the immortals had returned. Despite her ability, she'd kept her knowledge quiet. She'd seen firsthand what could happen if she started a movement on their behalf. That was how she had lost her twin.

So Kora had begun to produce fruit, vegetables, and herbs and used them to supply the local market. Others came to help, taking what she taught them and growing their own produce until the grocer was thriving. He had supplied her with seeds during the famine and their working relationship continued.

For those less fortunate, she'd assisted by giving much of what wouldn't easily sell to those in need while also providing families with seeds and seedlings to produce their own food.

All of this had drawn the attention of her local university who had, at first, overlooked her application. With news of a young woman bringing plants back to life, a spot had become available. She now had fulfilled her dream of attending university—even though it had come with some difficulty. Many still didn't take her seriously, and botany wasn't a subject considered pivotal until recent events. Educational opportunities were lacking at the university level. Kora was adjusting to teaching herself through her experiments instead of relying on others' knowledge. With the power of understanding plants at her beck and call, it was becoming easier to do so.

"Kora," her brother's call had her head snap up, her heart racing at the sound of his raised voice. The memory of her twin calling her name flashed across her mind. She got to her feet, ready to run when Michael came into view. "A letter arrived." He slid to a stop. "Momma wants you."

"A letter?" Her eyes widened as fear transformed into hope and twisted around her heart. Oxford had her application for three months now. Letters had recently been sent by two of her professors to vouch for her work ethic and potential.

"They gave it to Father at work. He phoned to tell her he was on his way."

Kora sighed, dusting herself off as much as possible. Mother wouldn't be thrilled to find her in trousers, let alone covered in dirt. But it made much more sense to wear casual attire compared to a dress with garden work.

Her polite and traditional mother always thought propriety was best. She did try, at least, to understand Kora and hold back on the judgment that used to plague their relationship prior to William's death.

Michael shifted on his feet, unable to stand still for long. His brown hair was windswept and for a brief moment Kora was pulled back to when her twin William had been Michael's age. They looked so similar. That ache of grief settled in her chest.

Her younger brother's brow furrowed. "What are you thinking?"

"A happy thought." A memory. "About William."

Michael gave a small chuckle. "I miss him."

"I know." She made sure to talk of him often to keep him present. Even if it was through memories that made her smile amongst the pain. It had been six months since their trip to Nekrós. Six months since she had done everything in her power to save his life. Six months since she had promised him that she would live.

"Any word from Shade?"

At the mention of the King of the Dead, Kora's smile wilted. "No, not yet."

"He will come soon. He always shows up when he's meant to."

Kora sat on the bench at the doorway and removed her boots. Her house shoes sat by the door, ready and waiting for her. "I hope you're right." In the past few weeks, Shade had become distant. A strange occurrence after the last five months of frequent visits. It's how she had begun to measure time. Every week, he would visit. Astraea, the Queen of the Pixies, would deliver letters from him in between. Then, once a month, he would arrive to take her to the Isles for her visit. Seven days was equivalent to a night in the mortal world. And for those seven days together, they would enjoy every moment side by side.

But at the end of her last visit to the Isles, she had noticed him watching her carefully. Not with want and the desire she had grown used to, but with concern and a touch of heartache. He'd told her nothing was wrong and yet...

"Kora, where are you?"

She winced at her mother's call. Mrs. Darling only had so much patience. She slipped on her house shoes and went inside to find her mother sitting at the dining table, sipping on her imported English tea and staring at a newly framed painting on the wall. At Michael's clomping steps, Mrs. Darling looked their way. She gave Kora a once over, pausing at the stains on her knees, then turned to her youngest. "You shouldn't be so heavy in your steps, Mikey honey. It's unbecoming."

Kora had to withhold the smirk at the nickname while Michael grimaced. "Mama, I asked you not to call me that. I'm not little anymore."

"You always will be to me."

It had been a new nickname—something that started a month after William's death.

"Nanny made baklava, Kora, if you would like some. How was your last day of school?"

Kora took a seat, curious as to why they were sitting in the dining room instead of the usual location in the living room. "It went well." She removed a piece of parchment from her pocket that she'd stuffed there earlier today. "Top marks in all my courses. And Professor Brighton offered to send another letter to Girton and Oxford as soon as possible to check on the status of my application."

"One should never turn their nose at the offer of help. What did you say?"

Her first thought was to grovel. "I thanked him for the offer." Uncertain how far to linger on this particular subject, she turned towards the painting on the wall. It was a lovely landscape of the Parthenon. "Did you do this one?"

Mother smiled. "I finished it." She stood, taking another sip from her cup, then pointed to the center of the painting. "If you look closely, you can see where William had left off. He had a few unfinished pieces." She brushed one of the strokes of white paint with her forefinger. "Most felt right to keep that way, but this one was similar to my style. It called to me, and I had to finish it."

William had often painted until his late teens when their parents had informed him that he was wasting his time and should concentrate on more important studies. Her parents regretted it now and found ways to accept their children's choices.

Kora brushed a tear from her cheek. They often snuck up on her. "He'd love that."

"I'm certain he would have. But enough about the painting." She turned her attention to Kora. "Tell me what else we can do to assist in your transfer to England?"

A few months back, this would have been a difficult subject between them. But now she knew that William wouldn't be left behind if she moved on. He'd live through her memories.

"Nothing." She sighed. "It's all about waiting now." And

whether either university was willing to take a chance on a young woman who wanted to study botany.

"You're a hero to Athens." Michael beamed. "Those schools would be silly to say no."

"He's right." Mrs. Darling stared at the painting for a moment longer. "You've helped so many with their gardens. Our community is thriving because of your green thumb."

Kora could hear the distance in her mother's voice. "Why are you sitting in here, Mother?"

She nodded toward the painting. "I miss him a little extra today."

Both she and her brother crossed the distance, taking a spot on either side of their mother. Kora grabbed her arm and leaned against her shoulder while Michael stared at the painting.

Kora scrutinized it. "Your styles here are very similar."

"They are."

"He would be happy to know you're painting again."

Kora ignored the tear that landed on her mother's sleeve.

"What is all this?" Mr. Darling's voice had them all turning quickly, as though having been found with their hands in the cookie jar.

Kora glanced at her mother as she wiped a tear from her cheek. "Reminiscing."

Father's expression softened, and he crossed the room and pulled his family into an all-encompassing hug. "Good." He squeezed them. "We need to do that from time to time."

Kora smiled, thankful her parents would still talk about William. She never wanted to forget her twin. "I heard there was a letter for me."

Father nodded and reached into his coat pocket to remove an envelope. "The courier stopped at the office first today and handed it to me then." He held it out towards Kora.

She could only stare at the linen parchment with her name written in an elegant script.

Michael began to jump up and down. "Open it!"

Her fingers were numb as she took the paper from her father. It was soft to the touch. Before opening it, she examined the scrawl on the front. It was beautiful calligraphy, but unfamiliar. "It's not from one of the universities, that's for certain." Her last touch of hope disappeared. Maybe tomorrow would bring news, but her curiosity was certainly piqued.

Mrs. Darling's brow rose as she looked from her husband to the envelope. "Open it, dear."

Hesitation stole over her. She didn't know what was within, but a weight settled in the pit of her stomach. Kora loosened a breath as she snapped the wax seal of a Greek temple.

When she removed the parchment, her mouth went dry.

"What is it?" Michael tried to jump up to grab it, but Kora kept it out of reach.

Gorgeous gold filament embossed the edges of an inked letter with words Kora had never expected. "It's an invitation."

# CHAPTER 2

"To what?" Mother asked.

There was something foreboding about the piece of paper. It felt heavier than it should have. A pulsing sensation prickled her fingertips, like a percussion beating against her skin. "A Starlit Masquerade, or so it's called. Hosted at the Stathos Mansion."

Before Kora could clutch it tighter, the invite slid from her fingers as her mother snatched it. Mother paused, her gaze suddenly distant. She wobbled slightly before her expression cleared and she caught her bearings.

"Are you all right, dear?" Father's brow rose in concern.

"Of course." Mother cleared her throat, then read aloud, "You are cordially invited, amongst all eligible bachelors and maidens of Athens, to attend a Starlit Masquerade on the seventh of June at Stathos Mansion."

Father's brow furrowed. "Who is the host?"

Mother shrugged. "I've never heard of him. Mr. Vasilis? Is the name familiar to you, dear?"

"No. And I'm not going to let my daughter saunter off to an unknown—" He paused as he took the invitation from his wife's hand. Kora frowned, titling her head to watch as the calm and collected Mr. Darling's face went giddy, his eyes bright as he examined the invitation. "Well, maybe I shouldn't jump to conclusions."

She exchanged a look with Michael who blinked at her. He had noticed the change too, but unlike Kora remained unconcerned. She had felt the power within the parchment and her parents were acting strange.

"Intriguing. This should be a wonderful opportunity." His voice was dream-like, filled with wonder. His fingers grazed the embossment on the edges of the paper. "You've never attended a ball like this one. You could meet the eligible bachelors all at once."

Kora's shoulders drooped, her thoughts shifting to Shade. Not that it took much to think about him since the immortal was nearly always on her mind. He was the only one who interested her, but how could he ever attend such an event even if she could tell him about it? Although she hadn't said it aloud, she knew she was in love with him. He'd only ever insinuated his feelings those months ago when he had battled Captain, who had taken back his true name as Theileus, the King of Immortals. There had been many opportunities during the last six months since her first visit to the Isles, but the words had remained unsaid. Kora had been too self-conscious and unsure to say them first. How does one tell an immortal that they love them when their time on this earth was much shorter? And what if Shade's feelings had shifted? Or were never as deep as hers?

She bit her lip but before she could check her expression, Mrs. Darling caught her eye. "Is there someone you know who may be there?"

Michael tried to reach for the letter, but Kora was faster as she nipped it from her father's hands. Whatever spell her parents were under, she didn't need that for her little brother. "No, Mother. I just don't have anything to wear...so I don't think I should go."

"Then it's time for a new dress." Her father made the announcement as if he wasn't the one who had turned down 'frivolous spending' on multiple occasions in the past few months. He was just as hesitant to believe that the worst was over.

Kora had hoped that the removal of the invitation would have been enough to bring sense back to her parents. She glanced over the careful script, looking for any hint of who had sent the invitation. She'd never heard of Mr. Vasilis. Stathos Mansion was owned by a family who had recently settled in Athens, but they didn't share the Vasilis name.

Something didn't add up.

"Dinner will be ready in a few minutes." Nanny bustled in, carrying a tray of dinner settings for the table. "If you'll excuse me, I'll prepare the table."

"Of course." Mother bustled them out of the room to get out of Nanny's way. As soon as they were all in the sitting room, Kora glanced at the staircase—an escape. "Why don't we discuss the masquerade tomorrow?"

"No." Father took a seat at the secretary on the far wall and opened the top drawer. He held out his hand for Kora, who hesitantly handed him the invitation. He removed the RSVP card from the envelope. "This is for your future. A future that has literally been handed to you. You will attend the masquerade. A response is requested as soon as possible, and we only have four days to prepare."

"That isn't much time," Mrs. Darling added, busying herself with her own mental checklist. Visible by the way she mumbled to herself and lifted one finger at a time for each item. "We have much to do."

Kora continued to watch them, the heaviness in her stomach doubling as her father handed off the quill and a parchment to Mrs. Darling to write a letter to the modistra. There was none of their usual concern that would come from a strange invitation. Not a touch of worry about the cost as her mother and father both prattled on about silk, traveling accommodations, and accessories. Couldn't her parents see there was something to be concerned about?

Obviously not, because her father was already finished with his response and was stuffing it into the envelope. His wax seal set was removed from the next drawer down, and he began the process of lighting the flame.

There was nothing else for it. Her parents may not have any qualms regarding the upcoming masquerade or its host, but she would find out what she could before then. She took the invitation from the table and placed it in her pocket to look for any hint of her parents' sudden excitement dwindling at its concealment. "Of course, Father."

"Good." Mother clapped her hands in excitement. "I'm certain we shall find you a suitable dress to wear. It won't be a problem at all."

Michael walked out with her as their parents spoke between themselves before leaving to find the messenger.

"What was that about?" Michael glanced up at her.

"Strange, that's what it was. Something wasn't right with the invitation."

Her brother stilled. "You can't go, Kora."

She crossed her arms. "I'll be fine. Don't worry about me." Though her words may not be true, she wouldn't worry Michael with her own trepidations.

"I'm not worried about you, but what will Shade think?" He mirrored her stance.

Kora bit the inside of her cheek, contemplating the validity of his question. Attending a ball was not unheard of—Shade would be fine. "Astraea should be visiting soon. I'll have her relay that I'll be going to a masquerade. But you must remember that Shade is an immortal." She swallowed, collecting herself before she could say the next words. "I care about him very much, but someone who lives for eternity and finally has some freedom may not want to be tied to me."

Michael, in all his innocence, scoffed.

Kora wished she felt the same way.

"He loves you."

"He's never said so," she whispered.

"Just because he doesn't say it doesn't mean he doesn't show it."

"Dinner time."

Nanny's announcement cut off any need for Kora to respond, because with the promise of food Michael was already running from the room, leaving her alone with her thoughts of the immortal. She cared deeply for Shade and there was no reason to be worried about her own intentions at the masquerade, but he deserved to know she was going. Otherwise, it would seem as though she was keeping something from him.

Though, with his recent absence, she wondered if he was having difficulty saying something to her.

After dinner—where her mother spent the entirety of the meal preening over dress ideas, and Michael was finally ushered to bed—Kora excused herself, feigning exhaustion from her last day of classes.

In the safety of her room, she leaned against the closed door and shut her eyes, releasing a long sigh.

"Family fun?"

Kora's head snapped up to find Astraea settled on her nightstand. The pixie's iridescent wings fluttered, and the pink tulip she wore as a dress swayed in the breeze from the open window. Even though she was only the size of Kora's palm, the Queen of Pixies always seemed larger than life.

Kora trotted towards her bed and sat down beside her. "Hello, Astraea. I had hoped to see you soon."

"Busy days coming up. The shift in the season takes a lot of work. Shade wanted me to inform you that he would be by in ten days for your next visit."

"Oh." She sat back, unsettled by the news. That was later than usual. "Did he give you anything for me?" A letter, she hoped but didn't say.

Astraea's brow rose. "No. Is there a problem?"

"I miss him, that's all." She meant it. The last month had felt much longer in his absence. The Isles had turned into a second home for her between the adventures she had with the Lost Souls, talking with Curly and Branch at the bonfires, and preparing souls before they passed from the Isle of Waiting. Deep down, she hoped Shade had missed her just as much as she missed him.

Astraea pursed her lips, and Kora wondered if there was something she wasn't telling her. Instead, she grumbled under her breath then gave her best smile. "I'm certain he will be here as soon as he can."

She thought of Michael's advice. But following the counsel of an eight-year-old didn't seem like the best idea. If he wasn't to visit, was there a reason to tell him about the masquerade?

"Anyway, is there anything to report about your power?"

Kora shook her head. "Nothing has changed. The plants still appreciate my care, but there hasn't been anything beyond them growing stronger, healthier, and faster—oh, I can check the nutrients in the soil now, but don't know if that is anything pertinent to consider. I might have been able to do it before and just didn't know it."

Astraea tapped her chin. "And no other strange things?"

"Not unless you count an interesting invitation. But nothing for my power to note." Well, there it went anyway, her subconscious making the decision for her. It seemed Kora couldn't help but torture herself.

"Invitation?"

Kora removed the parchment from her pocket. She'd

stuffed it in there so others couldn't touch it. "This arrived today. I think there might be something to it, though."

Astraea cocked her head. "Something to it?"

"A power. Do you sense anything?" Kora held it up so Astraea could read through it from top to bottom.

"You can sense something from this?"

"Yes."

The pixie frowned. "What type of power?"

"First there was a bit of a sensation that seemed to vibrate from it. Then my parents were adamant that I attend. For my mother, that's nothing new, but there had been a strange change to their countenance as soon as both of my parents touched the parchment."

"If I remember, though, your parents were very interested in your marriage prospects."

Kora couldn't deny that. "Yes, but my father normally isn't willing to buy a new gown at the drop of a hat. None of us know who the host is either. My father would usually want to know the person whom the invitation was from."

"Strange." She held her hand out. "May I take it with me?"

"Yes. Why?" Kora folded it up as small as she could for the pixie. With the way her parents had poured over every detail, Kora had no doubt that they had memorized it. "Is this name familiar?"

"No." At Astraea's touch, the invitation shrunk to her size, and she put it into the leaf-made pouch that hung at her side. "But the immortals have returned, and they have been withheld from their shenanigans for many years."

"They've been quiet, and as far as I've heard, there hasn't been anything to compare to the stories of old." Since their return six months ago, they had been remarkably quiet. Nothing like the stories Nanny had told her, or the escapades she had read about in her studies.

"Maybe not—yet." Astraea patted the pouch. "That

doesn't mean that they aren't biding their time. Just be careful."

Kora examined the pixie's face, looking for signs that she was hiding something. "Did you sense anything?"

"That's a complicated answer. I sense traces, but that could easily be the power you contain. You touched this letter too."

"But I don't have that much power."

Astraea rubbed a hand over her face, turning away. "That doesn't mean I can tell from this. Do you mind if I tell Shade the details?"

Kora's shoulders slumped. "I have nothing to keep from him."

Astraea stood and fluttered over, her wings like a dragonfly's as she patted Kora's cheek. "I know you don't, dear."

"Is there something he's keeping from me?" Or someone, she thought but couldn't ask.

Astraea sighed. "Shade has always been complicated. He doesn't mean to be, but he feels more than others. There is no other, if that's what you're asking. If that's not it, then you should talk to him."

"It's a little difficult to talk to him if he isn't here."

"I understand, but he is dealing with a lot of things as well."

"Is there something *you're* not telling me?"

The pixie sighed. "You will see him in ten days."

Kora feigned a smile. "In other words, you aren't getting involved."

Astraea chuckled as her wings sped up. "Correct." Then she whizzed from the room and out the window.

Kora sighed as she watched her pink dust disappear from sight.

# CHAPTER 3

Kora sat across from her mother as they rode down the cobbled path towards the modistra. The carriage was newly constructed judging by the strong leather scent and seats that didn't show any sign of wear. Plush velvet benches were encased by gold filigree with jet black trim. The Andravida horses pulling it were sleek. The months of proper food and diet evident in their prancing energy and healthy bay coat.

The modistra was only a ten-minute walk from their house. One Kora had made a few times since the modistra opened three months ago. And yet, today, her mother had not only hired a carriage, but had sent a messenger to schedule an appointment before they had even opened.

"We could have walked, Mother."

Mrs. Darling rolled her eyes. Actually. Rolled. Her. Eyes. Kora had to fight her jaw's reaction to drop in shock. "You're one of many invited to this masquerade. We can afford to show off a little bit."

Father would have said differently had his mind not been muddled by whatever power was within that invitation. Instead of the pragmatic response she had expected, he had countered that they should have ordered a car instead. She had hoped that her parents would be back to normal this morning. But whatever spell they were under would be in effect until the masquerade. That meant three more days of *this*. She didn't want to imagine if it could get worse.

Kora looked out the window to find families strolling along the stone walkway, bustling shops open with customers inside, and a printer's apprentice sweeping the front steps. In her lifetime, she'd only known desolation, dusty roads, and beggars. A mere six months and people had already begun to flourish and the city was showing that it would thrive.

The carriage came to a staggered stop. A footman opened the door, raising a hand to assist her mother before helping Kora out. He rushed ahead to open the door to the modistra, and the sound of raised voices spilled out. They walked in to find the modistra's assistant trying to calm two mothers and a daughter glowering in the corner.

"We were here first," the daughter snapped at Kora as she and her mother entered.

The two mothers began to bicker again, ignoring the young woman who glared at Kora.

"We have an appointment." Mrs. Darling lifted her chin and stared down her nose at the young brunette-haired woman whose brown eyes were pinched in disdain. "Do you?"

"It is first come first serve," the snotty daughter responded, crossing her arms over her lavender alatzas dress.

Kora's teeth clenched, and she took a moment to bury the overwhelming urge to slap her.

"It doesn't matter." Mrs. Darling tilted her head. "Our messenger was here prior to opening to schedule our time slot. If you were unable—"

"Mrs. Darling, you're a few minutes early." The modistra's assistant appeared from behind a cream curtain wearing an apron covered in pins. She pushed between the two angry parents without paying them any attention. "Miss Darling, if you will come with me, I'll escort you to a changing room where the modistra will be with you soon."

Kora's mother took a step forward. "I'm coming with—"

"No." The assistant shook her head, raising a hand to stop her. "We have a full house today, madam. Please wait here."

Kora was thankful that she wouldn't have to deal with the

chaos in the front of house as the others started to rage again. A quick glance over her shoulder, and Kora found her mother standing with a self-assured smile and the poised grace of a woman who had outsmarted others.

"I hope you don't mind that we only have a privacy divider. This masquerade has all the mamas in a bustle."

"Will you be attending the event?" She wondered if it was true that every available man and woman would be in attendance. Or, at the very least, invited.

Her freckles stood out as her cheeks pinked. "I hope to. Only if Miss Sophia has time to fashion something for me."

At the sound of the modistra's name, Miss Sophia appeared with her hair gathered in a bun on the top of her head in a pompadour with a few strands loose. Pins stuck out from the lace trimmed sleeves of her blouse and a measuring tape hung around her neck. "Oh, Miss Darling, good, good. Your dress is ready to be tried on, then we can check measurements."

Kora frowned. "Dress? But I haven't finalized anything yet."

Miss Sophia gave a small smile. "It was delivered with direct instructions that it was yours. I am to add a few embellishments and otherwise only confirm the fit is correct."

Kora glanced at the other dividers, hearing mutterings between patrons and the other assistants. "Did the others also have the same?"

Miss Sophia shook her head as she wrapped the measuring tape around Kora's waist. "No. Just you. Maybe you have an admirer?"

Here was another note to add to the strange and confusing list. The curious invitation, the response of the city, her parents' reaction, and now a beautiful dress. It was all very mysterious. If the immortals were at play, then who and why? "How busy has it been today?"

"Nonstop all morning. I've never seen such excitement before."

Miss Sophia turned to her assistant who was ready to write down the measurements. After she prattled off some numbers, she nodded and rehung her measuring tape over her shoulder. "Thea, take her back and assist her into her dress. I'll check in a few minutes after I get the others out of my store, or an appointment scheduled."

"Yes, miss." Thea gave a small curtsy, then gestured for Kora to follow her.

Sophia shook her head. "None of that, my dear. Formality is not necessary here." She patted the younger woman on her arm, then drew back the curtain that divided the two rooms and disappeared to deal with the squabbling mothers. Thankfully, Kora's mother was still grinning, her head held high.

"Here we are, miss." Thea led her towards the divider and pulled aside the curtain.

The moment she walked into the closed-off space, Kora's eyes landed on a shimmering silver gown. It looked like liquid metal. She ran her fingers along the fabric to find little pinpricks of silver and gold studding the skirt and bodice. She inhaled a slow breath as she took in the thin straps for sleeves, the way the dress would hug her curves before it flared out at her hips, to the open V-neck and deep slung back. "Where did this come from?"

Thea examined the dress from her place beside Kora. "It arrived with the morning messengers. At first, Miss Sophia thought it had been sent by your mother, but this fabric is unlike any other we have ever seen before. Our esteemed modistra has enough knowledge of our local distributors to know that they don't have access to such treasures. Whoever has been taken by you has exquisite and expensive taste."

Another note for Kora to consider about this strange occurrence. A foolish part of her hoped it was Shade that had commissioned the dress, but wouldn't he have visited if he knew about the masquerade? He wouldn't have made such a spectacle by including the entire city. Would he? "No one in Athens has ever made their interests known. Whatever or whoever this is, I can't imagine I've ever met them or have had the means to cross them."

Thea shrugged her lean shoulders. "Well, let's try it on, shall we?"

Kora slid from her layers of clothing until only her chemise remained. Thea shook her head. "With this dress, unfortunately there are particular undergarments necessary." She held up a piece of silk and lace that had both young women blushing. No bralette—just underwear that was nearly the same as wearing nothing at all.

After she slipped on the undergarment, Thea helped her slide the dress over her frame, and a chill ran down her spine as the fabric brushed against her skin. It felt otherworldly, and although there was no twinge of power that came from its touch this time, she knew it could not have been made by a mere mortal.

And it was scandalous. The front V-neck dipped mid chest. Thin straps covered by pieces of silk hung like a short cape and barely covered the dress's plunged back. A slit drew up her thigh, revealing skin from her ankle to her hip.

It was unlike any other dress she'd ever worn with full skirts and frilly sleeves. The dress hugged every curve and dip of her body.

"I can't wear this." Kora thought of her mother who waited in the main room and the countless others she would meet at the masquerade. If other attendees saw her in this, she would undoubtedly be the talk of the ball. Before she knew what to do, Thea turned her towards the mirror on the opposite wall, and every word of resistance disappeared. She felt powerful. Sophisticated. Absolutely stunning.

The silk fabric felt like a caress. The brush of air against her exposed skin had her heating from head to toe. Images of Shade and the way he would touch her filled her thoughts. How he would hold her against him. And a part of her ached. For him. For his presence. To know with complete certainty that he would be there.

And she swore to herself then that the next time she saw him, she'd tell him how his absence had made her feel.

As she left the store with her mother, she spotted a familiar face and waved at Ariana and her mother who crossed the street to meet them. "You're here?"

Kora's gaze trailed over her friend whose usually wild hair was pinned back with a dark blue ribbon so everyone could see her face. Her hazel eyes were bright and curious—how Kora imagined she was on her father's ship but never in town.

Ariana nodded and smiled at her mother. "May I have a moment?"

Both mothers began their own conversation as Ariana reached into the leather pouch at her side. "Did you see this?"

Kora glanced down at an invitation that nearly matched hers. Before Kora could discern the finer idiosyncrasies of the script, Ariana folded it again and tucked it away as if it were a sacred text.

"Yes." Kora met her friend's gaze, searching for a reaction to the strangeness of it all and was met with an ear-to-ear grin. "I did. I plan to attend. Do you?"

Ariana beamed. Brightly. In a way Kora had never seen the young woman smile. It even caused a passing man to give her a second glance, but instead of blushing at the attention, she gave a little wave.

"Yes," she said and grabbed Kora's hands. "This is so exciting. I cannot believe we will be at the party together. Or maybe I should have—we are both available young women."

Kora blinked as her nearly always composed friend squeezed her hands and gave a little hop in excitement.

"We are getting my dress fitted at noon. Papa thought I would prefer to be on the ship preparing for our end of the month launch, but this took precedence."

"Did your father see the invitation?"

Ariana quickly glanced at her mother. "Yes, but he didn't seem that impressed. Mama and I were giddy as could be. At least he agreed a new gown was necessary."

"I see." Another thought came to her—Father hadn't agreed until he touched the letter. "Did your father touch the invitation?" She glanced around for the man, knowing he'd stand out in the crowd.

Ariana tilted her head. "What an odd question to ask. Simply curious." She tapped her index finger to her temple. "No, I don't believe he did."

The merchant captain was observant and had seen things Kora could only imagine. Although, in the past few months, some could say the same thing about her. If they knew what she had been up to, that is. "Where is your father?" Although they were neighbors, it wasn't often that she saw him since his travels kept him busy.

"He'll be here any moment. He knew Mama couldn't be trusted with the budget." She leaned in and gave Kora a quick squeeze. "I'm so glad we will be there together," she whispered before turning towards her mother, leaving Kora gawking as all three women began to chat excitedly.

"My daughter doesn't like to go to dances."

Kora jumped at the gravelly voice. She glanced up to see Ariana's father beside her, his graying beard trimmed after returning from a trip with Ariana the previous week. The top hat upon his head still had some dust from lack of use.

"I know."

Kora peered at him from the corner of her eye. He stood

stoically, watching his wife and daughter with his mouth drawn taut and a piercing gaze. "Do you plan to attend this masquerade?"

"It seems that way." Kora waved at her mother who returned the gesture before turning to the others again. "I didn't have much say in the matter."

She could feel his attention on her. "You appear to have your wits about you."

"As do you."

He cleared his throat, turning back to the women. "They usually do not get excited about such events."

"It seems nearly the entire city is enthusiastic about the opportunities this masquerade could give them. Maybe Athens needs a reason to celebrate after years of famine." She glanced back towards her mother as the three women finished giving their goodbyes. It must be nearly time for Ariana's appointment.

He sighed. Loudly. "Be careful. The gods have been known to play games in the past."

"I'll watch out for her at the masquerade."

The merchant nodded. "I know you will," he agreed and then headed towards his family who were waving for his attention.

Kora raised a hand in farewell to her friend as her mother caught up and wrapped Kora's arm through hers. "You two will have such a lovely time. I'm glad Ariana feels confident enough to attend. Maybe she will finally find a respectable husband."

Kora bit her tongue. Her mother judged Ariana's parents for allowing her to travel with her father and speculated that she wouldn't be so anxious in crowds if she remained on land. But Kora knew that Ariana was an invaluable asset to her family's business and a knowledgeable navigator. One of the best.

If it wasn't for the fact that she was a woman, she would be highly sought after by every fleet.

"Maybe she will," Kora sighed though her thoughts had drifted. She had suspected that the immortals might be behind these strange occurrences, but why hadn't their magic worked on her if that was the case? And why was she the only one? Her own power couldn't have been strong enough to stop it, could it? Or was there something more to this whole fiasco?

There was only one way to find out. Undoubtedly, Kora was going to need her wits about her to get through this masquerade.

# CHAPTER 4

KORA BARELY SLEPT during the next two nights. On the evening before the masquerade, she tossed and turned, an ache settling in her core that couldn't be soothed. Heat slid over her skin at every touch of the blankets. At every graze of her skin. It was a need that felt like it could never be satiated. And it consumed her. It wasn't just anxiousness that had kept her up.

She turned and stared at the outline of the dress that hung from her armoire in the dim lantern light. It had arrived that morning, and her mother hadn't done the one thing Kora had expected—demand to see it on. She claimed it was for the reveal prior to Kora's departure. An oddity that must have to do with whatever was happening to the town. When she'd walked through the streets, residents preened more than usual. Flirtation happened openly. Families flaunted wealth that had previously been hidden.

The heat of summer was not the only thing rising.

"It's a beautiful dress."

Kora nearly fell out of bed. She flung off her blankets and was immediately on her feet. She turned and caught sight of the only man she ever wanted to see. His copper hair was windswept, and his dark pewter armor clung to his body. Those blue eyes danced with mischief and curiosity.

Except, he was not a man...

Immortal.

The King of Nekrós smiled at her. "Hello, Kora."

"You're here," she whispered as she closed the distance between them and wrapped her arms around Shade's waist.

He returned the embrace, holding her close and burying his head in her hair. Her eyes fluttered closed as he sighed against the sensitive skin of her neck. She leaned further into him, inhaling his scent of bergamot, memorizing the sensation he left behind as his lips skimmed her jaw. She bit back a moan as a heat curled low in her stomach.

"I've missed you."

It was an admittance she had only hoped to hear. Prior to the previous four weeks, neither of them had wanted to be apart for long. Sometimes, she would travel back with him for just a few days, returning before the mortal world had even hit midnight. The past few weeks of silence had been daunting.

"I've been right here."

He pulled back, and his smile held a touch of sadness. "I know. It's been a bit hectic lately."

"What has kept you away?"

"I'm having difficulty finding answers." He glanced over his shoulder at the dress. "Astraea mentioned you'd been invited to a masquerade."

She noted the change of subject. "Every available man and woman in Athens has been. Something hasn't been right since the invitation arrived."

Shade's brow furrowed. "Oh?"

"Everyone is excited. Animosity and competition have been rising and everyone is vying for attention. Any type of attention..." She wanted to talk about anything else though. A part of her didn't want to talk at all, her gaze lingering on his lips. He brushed his knuckles along her bare arm. He leaned in, kissing her forehead. Her cheek. Her body thrummed with need. She shifted from one foot to the other. "How long can you stay tonight?"

His movement paused. He wrapped his hand around hers and lifted it to kiss her knuckles. "Not long."

"Oh." She stepped in closer to him and grazed her fingers

against his arm. "I had hoped you could be here for a few hours. Or maybe I could come with you."

"I wish."

It was like a cold bucket of water had been poured over her. She took a step back and glared at him. Kora wanted to ask all the questions she didn't have the answers to. Why was he pulling away? Did he still care about her? Could he be bored of her already?

"That dress. Where did you get it?" he asked before she could voice her own question.

She frowned, her lips taut. One problem at a time. Maybe he had an idea of the identity of the host or who had sent the strange dress. "It had been specifically delivered to the modistra for me."

He let go of her hand and walked towards the dress to hover a hand over the fabric. "Interesting. And you don't know where it came from? Or from who?"

"No." She usually didn't try to make others jealous, but she needed to know if he'd react. "The modistra thought it was from an admirer."

"I didn't send it. Whoever chose it, did well." His brow furrowed. "There is something about it though..." He tilted his head. "And the mask?"

"We will receive it tomorrow upon our arrival. Why?"

"You're correct—this does sound strange."

Her jaw tightened, and she closed her eyes for a brief moment. "Shade, we need to talk. The thing is—"

"Who is the host?"

Kora's shoulders slumped. "I don't know them. An enigma it seems. We weren't given the finer details. His name is Mr. Vasilis."

"I see."

Shade turned and pressed a kiss to her cheek. "I'm going to see if I can find any answers. I'll see you soon."

"No, Shade—"

Then he was gone. A piece of her heart ached at his absence. And another emotion had clawed its way to the surface. Frustration.

And with that frustration, another ache grew. Yearning. Desire. Want. She stared at the spot Shade had been just moments before. Kora stomped her foot with a grumble, fists forming at her side.

A knock at her door had Kora scrambling back into bed, but she wasn't fast enough to settle herself before a crack of light illuminated Nanny who poked her head in. "Are you all right, dear?" She looked at Kora from head to toe. "You look upset."

"Everything is fine, Nanny. I guess I'm a little nervous about tomorrow." She grabbed hold of one of her pillows and stuffed it in her lap to have something to fidget with.

"The masquerade?"

"Yes. It seems like a lot of trouble when we don't know the host. I know the famine may be over, but the spending and frivolities...it seems like a lot."

Nanny peered over her shoulder before entering and closed the door behind her. "It's a once in a lifetime opportunity. Or so your parents have said."

Kora tilted her head, hearing words left unsaid. "What do you think?"

"It's not my place—"

"It is if I ask."

Kora could barely make her out in the dim lantern light beside her bed. Nanny stepped closer, her warm smile a comfort. "I think it is unexpected that your parents would send you so willingly to an unknown host's home. You are a smart young woman, though, so I trust that you will make the decisions that are best for you."

"What if I don't have a choice on whether or not to go?"

Nanny smiled. "Is he going to be there?"

"He?" Her throat went dry.

"The one that has been distracting you as of late. Don't think I haven't noticed a change in you. It was subtle at first. I thought it was because of William." Her smile softened at the mention of her late brother. "Then it shifted."

Kora wanted to deny it. But this was Nanny who had raised her, and she knew her to be trustworthy. Even in matters of the heart. "Do you think my parents noticed?"

"No. And like I said, I know you to be wise. Even with your heart, I suspect."

"I hope so." The words came out as a whisper. "No, he won't be there. He's not local to Athens." Although it would be nice to talk to someone about her relationship and even more to tell them who Shade was, how could she admit that she was in a relationship with the God of the Dead? "He was not invited."

"Did you invite him?"

That forlorn frustration reappeared, but Kora tried to keep it from her expression. "I haven't really had the chance to."

"I see." Nanny crossed the room and took Kora's hands in hers, uncurling the fists still tightly folded. "Your heart and your mind may be at war at times, but use them both tomorrow night. If they agree, then you know you're on the correct path." She kissed Kora on the top of the head and headed towards the door.

Kora watched her retreating figure and considered what her heart and mind were telling her now.

Currently, they were not in agreement.

# CHAPTER 5

IT WAS the height of summer. The thin embroidered cream wrap Kora's mother had gifted her for the evening covered her shoulders. She thought that as soon as she had walked down the stairs in the scandalous silver gown, her parents would come out of their trance and stop her from walking out of the house.

But as much as she wanted her parents to put their feet down and scold her for the lack of material covering her body, none of that happened.

"You look absolutely exquisite." Her parents stood at the bottom step, right off the foyer leading towards the front door. Mrs. Darling was leaning against her father as they watched her walk down the stairs. If Kora hadn't considered something amiss before, saying such a thing while Kora's leg appeared through the slit of the dress would have confirmed it.

Kora hid her grin as she stopped at the bottom of the steps, and even though she knew he was spelled too, she still expected her father to say something. He just grinned back at her.

Despite her worries and discomfort, she had to admit that there was something empowering about wearing the dress without judgment.

"The car is waiting for you." Her father held out his arm for her.

"What?" Kora balked. "You didn't need to spend money on such a thing. A carriage would be completely appropriate."

"Maybe, but it wasn't us." Mr. Darling took her to the

door where the black pristine automobile waited. "Mr. Vasilis sent it."

Kora stared at the automobile waiting for her. A man dressed in a crisp black suit stood at the back door of the car, holding it open for her.

A shudder slid down her spine. Intrigue, fear—she was having a hard time differentiating between the two.

Her father led her towards the car while her mother stood at the doorstep. Kora looked down at the mosaic owl under her feet and thought of Shade. The owl stared back, as if it knew she was torn. She wanted to have all her questions answered and knew the only way that would happen was to get in the car. Intuition told her to turn around now and return to her room. Wait for Shade.

But she wasn't that type of woman. She slid off her father's arm and into the car's leather seat. The driver had put up the canopy and turned the hand crank before taking the driver's seat in front of her. Kora ensured her dress was fully within the vehicle before her father closed the door. She'd never been in such a contraption before, and she couldn't help the jittery excitement, even if she was aware of every stutter and pop of the motor.

Mr. Darling patted the door. "Have fun tonight."

The last words she expected from the man. "Thank you, Father."

The driver turned around in his seat. "There is a gift for you, miss."

Then as the car sputtered forward, Kora shifted to find an olivewood box with a red ribbon beside her seat. She opened the lid and gasped, the sound covered by the rumble of the automobile. Inside, on a bed of crimson velvet, was a gorgeous black mask. It would do nothing to cover her identity with its metal wires that twisted to form arrangements of wildflowers and lupines that would curl around her eyes and over her nose.

Before she removed it from the box, she took a letter that had been placed beside it and unfolded it.

*To Kora Darling,*

*It is an honor to have you attend this inaugural masquerade at the behest of Mr. Vasilis. Upon consideration, he's chosen you as his guest of honor for tonight's festivities. Please accept this mask as a token of his appreciation.*

*Sincerely,*
*Mr. Diamandis*

It was short and sweet. Not a hint as to who their host truly was. But what worried her more was being the 'guest of honor.' Why her? She should have begun a parchment of notes in an attempt to decipher the clues jumbled in her head, because they didn't make sense.

She picked up the mask, unable to discern the type of metal with the limited light. Fingers grazing the cold metal, Kora sensed power that reminded her of the invitation. With a furrowed brow and only a moment of hesitation, she placed the mask against her face, then tied the black satin ribbon behind her head. It was a perfect fit. As if the creator had her face to form it to.

They passed Thaelius' temple, and she wondered if the King of the Immortals was content now that everything was as it should be. As much as he had disliked his short-term role in Nekrós, she had little doubt that he wouldn't last long quietly living on Synnefos—the clouded Mount he ruled from. She had briefly suspected him of being the masquerade's host, but this didn't seem like something he would do.

She inhaled sharply, staring at the box in her lap. Before her adventures in the Isles, Nanny had told her stories of the havoc the immortals had once caused. Shade too had said that their absence was as much a blessing as a curse. Sure, the land and world itself had healed upon their return, but if they thrived on chaos...

She fumbled with the letter, staring at the name of their host. Which one of the many immortals could he be? And if she was the guest of honor, what did they have planned?

Thoughts of the immortals drifted away as the illuminated mansion came into view. Lights danced through windows, and lanterns hung from the boughs of the trees that dotted the landscape leading up to the entrance. Kora bit her lip as the car came to a stop at the bottom of a staircase. White pillars cordoned off the arched doorway. Men in full military regalia stood on either side of the steps, at attention with hands clasped behind their backs. They all wore masks made of different materials. The driver opened her door, holding out his hand so Kora could step down. As soon as her heeled shoes touched the ground, that *other* sensation stole through her skin, through her bones, to her blood. Her own power, usually quiet and dampened, shuddered.

The driver let go of her hand, and Kora noted his vacant expression as he gave a half bow before returning to his vehicle. Once again, she considered getting back into the car and going home, but she doubted the driver would do as she asked.

And she still needed to know.

As her toe touched the first step, she balked as the attendants all snapped their heels together and straightened with arms tight at their sides. She glanced behind her, towards the car driving away. She looked around, wondering if she was the last to arrive but the sound of a carriage coming up the drive was her only sign that other guests were still arriving.

With a fortifying breath, she lifted her chin and took each

step slowly, gaining a touch more confidence as the eyes of the welcoming party watched her ascend.

At the entrance, she considered knocking on its closed doors, wondering if she was to wait for one of the gentlemen behind her to open the door when both doors opened inward, revealing a vast foyer with tall ceilings and Grecian pillars. In awe, she entered, shoes clicking on the marble floors as she turned in a small circle and gaped at the diamond encrusted chandelier.

"It's beautiful, isn't it?"

Kora gasped, whirling around to find a sophisticated gentleman standing in the entrance of a hallway.

A mask of navy satin covered half of a clean-shaven face, showcasing full lips that lifted into a mischievous grin. Salt and pepper hair brushed his shoulders in soft waves. "I didn't mean to startle you. Kora Darling, I presume?"

"Yes," she swallowed. "And are you—"

He shook his head before she could finish her question. "No, I'm Mr. Diamandis. I will escort you the rest of the way. He will meet you in the main hall."

"The rest of the way?"

His grin shifted to a smirk. "It's a little quiet here for a ball, don't you think?"

It was, but Kora couldn't let him know she was flustered. "Lead the way."

He gave a small bow, then turned and held his arm out in a crook.

Kora slid her arm through his. "Have you known Mr. Vasilis long?"

From the corner of her eye she saw the wrinkles at his mouth shift, aged skin smoothing to unflawed bronze while his thin face morphed to a feminine heart shape with full lips. Kora blinked and turned abruptly away as his appearance changed back to an elderly man.

He didn't notice her confusion as he waved his free hand. "I've known him nearly my entire life. We grew up together."

"Whereabouts are you from?"

Kora tried to sound as nonchalant as possible as she scanned the hallway and followed the golden threaded rug.

"Here and there," he chucked to himself. "Have you traveled much, Miss Darling?"

Someday she hoped she might be able to see more beyond Athens. A pang gnawed at her chest—six months ago she would have never considered leaving her home. The place that held her memories of William. Now she knew he was with her no matter where she was. "No. Not really. I hope to visit England soon."

"I see, and what is drawing your attention across the sea?"

As they walked, she noted there were no adornments on the wall. No portraits of the owner, families, or even landscapes. It was a blank canvas of clean white walls.

"My studies." She prepared for the usual skepticism that came with such an announcement. "Our local universities don't have many options for women. Many still don't allow us to attend."

"Oh, and what is a woman of your stature interested in studying?"

At his response, she glanced at him. "The sciences. In particular, botany." She hoped that she kept her voice even.

"Intriguing." His brow rose in consideration.

"Why is that?" She had dealt often with the doubt of men. The first who had ever believed in her had been her brother. Then Shade.

"Not many women chance stoking the fire of their social status to study. They prefer to fall within the norm. Maybe this is one reason Mr. Vasilis has noticed you."

Would she be able to get something out of this man

regarding their enigmatic host? "And does he know that I study?"

Mr. Diamandis shrugged. "I wouldn't know."

"But you said that you're his closest friend...and welcomed me at the door to find out more about me. Don't you think it's polite to share a little about the man who I'm meant to meet this evening?"

The sounds of instrumental music and chatter heightened as they drew closer to the set of double doors. She'd barely paid attention to how many doors they had passed. The hallway had, at one time, felt unending. Except for the thrum she felt from the mask, she couldn't detect any further power from within the room.

Mr. Diamandis came to a stop and leaned towards her. "Here's a little something to know about him." She couldn't help it as she moved closer as he whispered, "He's no mortal man."

Before Kora could respond, the doors flew open, and all the guests turned towards her. Her arm dropped to her side and she inhaled deeply as she stared back at the rapt room. She turned to her guide only to find that Mr. Diamandis had disappeared. Others began to whisper behind hands or into ears as they watched her.

The room itself was layered in darkness. Candles were settled on eye-level tables and on candelabras that encircled the room alongside seating areas. A dimly lit alcove was created under a balcony overlooking the dance floor. High above the revelers was a domed ceiling of starlight. The most stars Kora had ever seen in her life.

A figure broke through the crowd, drawing her attention. He was exquisitely dressed head to toe in black. The only exception was his mask.

Kora gasped as he stalked towards her. Handsome. Strong, shaven jaw. A wave of copper hair hung over his brow, grazing a crimson mask shaped into rose buds. He wore ink-black trousers that fit like a glove, and a suit jacket that was cut to perfection over his defined shoulders and tapered to his lean waist. Confidence graced each step as the other guests parted to allow him to pass.

He stopped before her and bowed, but Kora could only stare as the music stopped.

Shade peered up at her as he straightened and grinned. "Hello, Kora Darling."

# CHAPTER 6

SHE SWALLOWED, staring into sky blue eyes nearly as familiar as her own. Any attempt to piece together what she was seeing went against everything she knew. "What is this?"

His grin widened. "Dance with me?"

Kora peered at her surroundings. Everyone seemed to watch with bated breath—and thus far, she didn't recognize any of those who looked back at her. Questions and thoughts rushed through her mind, but not a single one grounded her to the moment. Nothing familiar. Even if the man before her should be.

She took his outstretched hand, and a wave of floral soap shocked her senses. "Yes."

He straightened, holding her in his firm yet gentle grip as he led her towards the dance floor. He lifted her hand, keeping nearly an arm's length between them. A heaviness settled on Kora's shoulders as dozens if not hundreds of eyes bored into her, watching her every move as he came to stop and faced her. Kora placed her hand on his forearm, the other at his shoulder.

With a nod from their host, the orchestra settled on a small stage in the center of the room and began an unfamiliar melody. Kora was swept up into a waltz—a dance she thankfully knew—careful to follow each of his steps. Others joined them while some remained to observe.

Kora glanced over the crowd for someone she knew. Something to hint as to what was happening. Diamandus' appearance had changed. And so did some of the guests. Kora's head spun at the fluttering changes around her. And this man she danced with...

"What is this?"

He pulled her slightly closer. "A masquerade. In your honor, I might add."

Roses burned her nose. Not the familiar scent of bergamot.

With their bodies nearly pressed against each other, she looked for the discrepancies, uncertain if he'd pull away once she revealed the truth. This was not the man she loved. Her dance partner's image shifted to dark brown hair, tan skin, and eyes a forest green before settling back to Shade's copper hair. His blue eyes.

That thrum of power that echoed the invitation pulled at her now. There was a staccato to the rhythm, one that didn't match the notes she knew to be Shade's. "Who are you?"

His chest brushed hers. "You don't recognize me?"

"You're not Shade, so let's not play as if I don't know him."

The immortal—because there was no denying his power's signature now—chuckled. "That was faster than I expected."

"Oh, and when did you think I'd figure it out?"

"A mortal?" He whirled her around and dipped her, dramatically curving her body in an arc before bringing her upright again. "Either not at all, or when morning came."

"Morning?"

Heat pooled in her stomach as he dipped his head to her ear. "You're not that innocent to not know what I'm inferring, are you?" The warmth of his breath curled along the sensitive skin of her throat. "Tangled sheets. Twisted limbs. Bare skin," he purred the words quiet enough for only her to hear as the others danced around them. "Maybe at that moment you would come to the realization."

Her mouth pursed tightly, and her grip dug into his arm.

There was no way she would be sharing a bed with him. Whoever he was. "I must be smarter than you expected."

"Hm. Maybe it is that. Or possibly there is something else about you?"

Appearances changed again. This time she spotted a student she'd passed in the university halls dancing with a blond who she had discussed planting asparagus with a week ago at the market. A nobleman who had once been a suitor danced with a young man she didn't recognize. As she watched them, he shifted from the pocked marked young man with greasy hair to a well-dressed, styled, and clear-skinned bachelor.

She brought her attention back to the immortal before her. "Who are you? Really?"

"Who do you think?"

She'd considered her studies of the immortals. "There are a few options with the power you possess."

"There are?"

Kora nodded, considering the little she knew about him already. "A trickster."

"Oh—was that meant to be hurtful?" His mouth tilted at the corner.

"I doubt you took it as such," she grumbled.

The other corner rose. "True."

"You've invited all of the available young women and men —so you must have something to do with lust, at the very least."

"Interesting. Go on."

With their absence for nearly fifty years, the stories of the gods had grown quiet as time had passed. She'd spent some time studying who they were, but there was a lot of information to sort through, and she was by no means a scholar on the matter. She remembered the image of dark brown hair. The piercing green eyes. The sharp angle of his jaw. His insinuation about a night with him. The way everyone had been acting in the past few days. Her eyes widened, and she thought of some of the stories most discussed by her professor. The man had been a romantic at heart. "Velos," she breathed. The God of Desire.

His smile grew. "No wonder he likes you."

"Who?"

"Monos."

Shade. The name he left behind more than fifty years ago —when the meaning of the word was what he felt the most. Of course she had researched him when she had the chance. There was unsurprisingly little on him since many feared death. Just his true name, that he resided within the Isles of Nekrós, and worked alongside Télos who retrieved the dead. "He goes by another name now."

"Oh, I know. But you know what his original name meant, correct?"

She ground her teeth. There was no doubt he wanted her to say it aloud, but she wouldn't. *Alone*. "It's not who—"

"He is?" Velos shook his head, finishing her sentence. "I invited him tonight, you know? I wanted to see the couple who had saved the mortal world and the woman who freed us."

That ache in her chest that was becoming all too familiar cracked open again. But she couldn't think of words. Didn't want to ask...

"He couldn't attend, it seems. Or, at least, he didn't bother to reply."

As of the previous night, he had known she would be in attendance. He'd kept this from her. Had even acted as though he knew nothing of the masquerade and made her look like a fool. "He's busy." A pitiful excuse, and Velos knew it.

"Then let's dance and forget all your worries, your cares, concerns, and even your dreams. Tonight is meant for frivolity and passion." He swooped her in another arc, and when they straightened, she was pressed tightly against his body. A small gasp slipped from her as he gripped her chin and his gaze flickered from her lips to her eyes. "You're stunning and shouldn't be ignored. I'll make certain of that. Wait for me."

He stepped away and it was as though he was eaten up by the crowd. She took a step back to catch her balance. Her head felt addled, confused. And her heart...

They weren't aligned. To have someone who looked like Shade speak his name—his true name of loneliness—she ached for him and for herself.

She turned and the shifting faces of the dancing crowd nearly had her tripping over her own feet. Though Velos had asked her to wait for him here, she wouldn't. So, with little care for the immortal who was pulling the strings, she zigzagged through the crowd.

Despite having the answer to who their host was, it still didn't make sense. Why was *she* here? What exactly was the reason for all of this pomp and drama?

Wine goblets passed by, filled nearly to the brim with red liquid that remained remarkably still on the server's tray. As she retrieved one, she caught sight of a fellow classmate and lifted her glass in greeting. He cocked his head, blond hair grazing his plain white mask. He watched her with confusion before sauntering towards her with a self-assured expression twisting his features. "Hello, lovely."

Kora brow rose. "Nathaniel?"

He nodded with a pleased smile. "Oh, you know my name. I'd like to know yours too."

"You do know it."

Nathaniel stepped in closer and reached for a curl that hung by her ear. Kora jerked away, confusion shifting to a glare as she took a step back. "What are you doing? You know me. It's me, Kora Darling." This was the most awkward interaction she could remember. Her stomach, a little queasy at his reaction, had her putting the goblet in her hand aside.

The young man snickered. "You look nothing like her. Good luck. She's one of the most—"

"Excuse me," Kora cut him off. "I prefer you not to fill in that blank." Good or bad, she didn't need to know. "And it *is* me."

Nathaniel ground his teeth, his smile fading to annoyance. "I know Kora. It's wrong of you to attempt to impersonate such a lovely and wise woman. I should—"

Kora touched her mask, no longer listening to his rant as he went off on a tangent about decency and decorum. The mask thrummed with power beneath her fingertips. Velos' had been shaped into roses—the flower associated with his station as God of Desire. Hers with wildflowers, and as her fingers curved along the lupins, she noted that some held little skulls within their petals. "Excuse me."

She whirled around and moved through the crowd towards the door. A need for fresh air and to catch her bearings had her staggering. Bodies shoved into her, most continuously shifting and changing appearances. A blue dress changed to purple then back to blue again. Flamboyant coats turned to black then to bright green. It was a menagerie of colors, like a kaleidoscope twisting and turning. Someone cursed as she fell into them and she muttered apologies, attempting to keep her head down and ignore the dizziness that had her stumbling into another.

"Careful," someone snapped.

Tears stung her eyes as she looked up for the exit, uncertain which direction to go. "Sorry."

A familiar laugh had her stumbling when she attempted to stop and was pushed from behind. "Hey, watch where you're going."

Kora ignored them, looking in the direction of a sound she

knew by heart. One full of happiness and curiosity. One of her favorite sounds. Except he wasn't meant to be here.

Just above the crowd, copper hair caught her eye. Her brow furrowed. Eyes narrowed. And as the man turned his portly face morphed into a defined jaw. The shoulders edged back, carrying the burden of the world but confidence with it.

Then he turned to face her and their eyes met. Blue like a bright sky. Shade smiled. She knew it was him. That's when she saw the company he kept. Three young women and one gentleman—and each were hanging onto his story like he was their only chance for water. For life.

And as he tilted his head, his shape changed again into the unknown man. People passed between them, blocking her view. She moved side to side, then stood on her tip toes to see through the crowd. When they moved aside, Shade was gone.

# CHAPTER 7

KORA CIRCLED THE CROWD, hoping she would run into him. But as soon as she made it to where Shade had been, he and those he had been speaking with had dispersed. She hadn't paid close enough attention to what they looked like—although, with guests' continuously changing identities, she didn't know if she could recognize them even if she had.

Could it have really been Shade? If so, why had he disappeared so quickly? Had he been a figment of her imagination, or had it been someone who looked like him? Or was Velos continuing to wear his face?

Kora's shoulders slumped as she turned in a circle, hoping he'd appear through the chattering groups and dancing crowd.

"Kora?"

She stopped and turned to find a young man staring at her with concern etched on his features. "Excuse me, who—"

His image shifted and where a strange young man had stood was her best friend. "Ariana?"

"You can recognize me?" She grabbed Kora's arm in a tight, firm grip.

When her features shifted again, Kora rolled her eyes at the sensitivity of the magic. "Come with me."

She took hold of Ariana's arm and nearly dragged her under the balcony. Kora turned to her friend and let her go. "Take off your mask?"

Ariana tried to pry it off. "It won't come off."

Kora attempted to take off her own, then Ariana's. The masks resisted as though they had become a second skin.

"Kora, what's happening?"

"There's some kind of magic at play."

"What if we are stuck like this forever? We're trapped." Panic rose in her friend's voice, her fingernails prying at the edges of her mask.

She took Ariana's hands, gripping them tight to stop her fumbling. "That won't be the case," Kora whispered, glancing about the room for somewhere better to hide. She wouldn't let that happen. She headed towards a wide marble staircase with an iron railing leading upwards in a dramatic arc towards a balcony. Ribbons of silver, gold, black, and white dangled from the edge of the dome ceiling. Some guests had begun to wrap the ribbons around their bodies, moving with the fabric as though dancing with a partner.

Instead of climbing, she led Ariana into a little alcove under the steps. By the time they stopped, her friend's breathing had become erratic.

"Look at me."

Ariana did, eyes wide. Or his. It was hard to tell as Velos' power radiated through the room. "Why...is...this..." Ariana couldn't finish her sentence between each gasping breath. Ariana leaned against the wall, nearly knocking her head on the stucco if Kora hadn't jerked her into her arms in time. Unable to carry her weight, she lowered down to the ground with Ariana's head buried in Kora's neck.

"Oomph." Kora felt the moment she fell unconscious, her body like lead as she crumbled against her. "Ari? Ariana, wake up."

Footsteps alerted her just as a man and woman came around the corner, and Kora glared as they paused to take in the scene of what appeared to be a woman and a man hiding in a precarious position.

"They beat us to it," the man said and whisked the woman away.

"Well, that was awkward." Kora shook her head, rubbing her friend's back in circles and frowning over the tightness of the corset on Ariana's green silk bodice. Before she could decide whether to loosen the strings, Ariana let out a moan and covered her face with her hands.

As Kora settled her against the wall and looked her over, Ariana blinked her eyes rapidly. "How do you feel now?"

Ariana pressed a hand to her chest, regulating her breathing as she paid attention to the beat of her heart—a process Kora had seen her use before. With a glance around the wide marble alcove, she turned her attention back to Kora. "Why did I come here?"

"You were excited a few days ago."

"I know. Or, at least, I vaguely remember that. But I still don't know why. I hate these things."

Kora grinned. "When did you come back to your senses?"

Ariana sat up, fixing her wrinkled and bunched floral skirt, obviously able to see them as Kora could at that moment. "As soon as I arrived and put on the mask—then I desperately wanted to leave. But before I knew it, I was whisked inside by a group of guests. They were so excited, and I froze, just moving with them. You were the first face that I recognized. I tried to find you amongst the crowd and I saw a few friends, but they acted like they didn't know me and told me to leave them alone. Maria called me a rude and presumptuous beast."

Kora winced. "To them, you look like a man."

"What?" Ariana's eyes widened and, for a brief second, she went so pale that Kora was worried she was about to faint again.

Kora gripped her friend's arm to ground her. "The mask. Or that is what I think is the culprit behind our changing identities."

Ariana bit her lip. "This doesn't make sense."

Of course it didn't. Ariana hadn't spent days with immortals, nor fallen in love with one.

Kora straightened, assisting Ariana to her feet. "I know. But even your dad wondered if the gods were involved."

Ariana stared at her. "I need out of here, Kora. I can't handle this."

"We can find a place for you to hide." There must be rooms upstairs in this gigantic mansion. Failing that, she could always escort her to the front door. They weren't prisoners within the house...at least, she hoped not.

"No. We need to stay together." She swallowed.

Kora remained hidden in the shadows along the edge of the ballroom, steering her friend and keeping them both from view of the crowd. In the time they had been behind the stairs, the music had taken on a new cadence, as had the mood in the room. With their identities hidden, the guests were becoming more brazen. Anonymity lowering their inhibitions.

Or, more likely, Velos had something to do with it.

String instruments made sharp trills. The flute was short and harsh. Couples were pressed together on the dance floor. And Kora turned to find Ariana gawking.

"Who is this, Kora?" she whispered. "What power do they possess?"

"The God of Desire. Or, at least, I think it's only him. I don't know if the Triad is here."

"The Triad?" she asked as they continued to maneuver around the outskirts of the room.

"There are three within the same sect. Velos, The God of Desire, Thélo, the God of Lust, and Áxios, the Deity of Love. If all three are here—I can't even imagine what trouble we will be in," Kora whispered.

In her studies, she had found a lot of information about the Triad. People were obsessed with the concept of love, so the time and energy put into researching the Triad had resulted in many studies and even more speculation. Some stories painted them as the villains—those who inserted themselves in the middle of relationships, creating rifts and drama. Others considered them heroes and the reason they had found their one true love. However, it was most often a problem when all three of them acted together.

"Is this just a game to them?"

Kora shrugged. She knew there was something bigger afoot. And as the guest of honor, it had something to do with her. And likely Shade too. "I don't know."

"And how do you know all of this?"

Kora nearly stumbled, catching herself on the wall as they neared the doorway. She paused there to consider how honest she should be before turning towards her friend. "Our host spoke to me. Danced with me."

"I thought I saw you." Ariana's gaze widened. "Why did he choose to dance with you?"

Could she tell her friend everything she knew? They may be able to uncover the answers quicker and then get out together. Kora would not walk out that door until she understood the reason for all of this. She needed to know why her city was turned upside down and why Velos had chosen her as his latest plaything.

"Oh, there you are."

Kora twisted around to find the god in question. He was no longer in Shade's form, but there was no doubt who stood before her. Velos was handsome—even in her current predicament, she couldn't deny that truth. He wore a deep navy suit with swirled embroidered embellishments on the lapels that played with the color of the crimson rose mask. Between his full lips, rugged jaw, and green eyes just visible under a wave of dark brown hair, he stood with a sense of confidence that screamed power. "Velos."

Ariana moved alongside her, and although she was

undoubtedly screaming on the inside, she stood defiantly and lifted her chin. "What is this all about?"

Velos' brow rose. "Who are you?"

"Her best friend. Now, who are you?"

"Best friend. Hmm...and you can recognize your friend?"

"Yes." Ariana crossed her arms.

"I see." He lifted his hand and snapped his fingers.

All sound stopped. Everyone froze.

And then Kora screamed.

# CHAPTER 8

ARIANA WAS as stiff as a corpse—if a corpse could remain standing. With wide eyes, and a glazed over expression, Ariana turned towards the double doors that swung open.

Kora waved her hand in front of her friend's face. "Ari?"

Ariana didn't respond. Didn't seem to even realize Kora was there. Then she started to walk with stiff arms and legs. She moved as though she wasn't even in her own body anymore.

Guests walked towards the door. An army of jilted movements in rows. Rigid as a tree, and unbendable as steel. Kora moved in front of Ariana and tried pushing against her body. "Let her go."

Velos appeared beside her, watching her futile attempts. "Isn't this what you wanted?"

"What do you mean?" She pushed again, Kora's boots sliding against the smooth floor as Ariana continued forward, undeterred. "I don't want her to walk out like this."

Velos sighed, then pulled Kora aside. She struggled against his hold and watched one person after another walk towards the double doors that led towards the exit. Her attention snagged on the last person, watching as the door snapped closed behind them. She searched her surroundings and gasped as illusions of people appeared from thin air, and then began to interact with each other as though hadn't just left. "Are they here or not?"

At some point during the parade of departures, she'd

stopped struggling. She didn't remember when. "What did you do?"

Velos let go of her. "Those who should leave have now left."

"Where is my friend?" Kora turned and grabbed Velos by the lapels of his pristine coat, twisted, and got inches from his face as she summoned all her rage. "Where did she go? Tell me now, or I'll—"

He grinned. "Feisty. Now, shut your mouth."

Kora's mouth snapped shut. She tried to open her jaw and when she couldn't, considered ripping him to shreds. Glaring at him as she held him in place, she knew there was little she could do to an immortal. He shifted his attention to whatever or whoever was behind her. "She's perfectly safe."

Her gaze hardened and narrowed. "Where is my friend?"

"Let me go and I'll tell you. You're starting to draw attention."

"I could care less. That's what this is all about, isn't it? You want attention after years of hiding away." She didn't look over her shoulder to see who watched. Didn't care who remained. Ariana's safety wasn't something she would play with.

He sighed. "I did not bring her any harm. She will safely return home to her bed, sound asleep, and will think this was all a dream."

Kora loosened her hold, but only slightly. This is what she wanted. What Ariana wanted. The undead way her friend looked had been terrifying. "Do I have your word?"

"Yes." He grinned.

"Prove it."

He tilted his head, appraising her. "I'm loyal to a fault."

"That doesn't prove a thing."

"It does for me." He held his head up and held her glare. "I promise, upon my honor, that if anything befell your friend you have the right to curse my name to another fifty years of imprisonment. Because I wasn't in hiding. I was imprisoned, like many others." Velos' features hardened, those full lips forming into a thin line and that gentle brow furrowing. "Most of us are curious about you, Kora Darling. Who you are. How have you achieved what no one else could? Be glad I'm the first to find you."

"Why?"

With preternatural speed, she was pinned against the wall and their breath mixed together as he leaned in. Something she didn't want to name stirred within her. "Many of us want to thank you," he whispered into her ear, causing goosebumps along her neck. "Others know you're *his* weakness. They are either angry with him for their long-term *hiatus* or never liked him to begin with and have searched for a way to break the King of the Dead."

"He doesn't have a weakness."

"That's where you're wrong." He nuzzled against her throat, hot breath tickling the skin on her neck. "You smell divine. Did you know that?" It wasn't Velos' voice, but Shade's.

As if on instinct, her body arched towards him.

He chuckled. "Interesting."

His hot breath against her skin had her body warming in response. He didn't touch her, but she wouldn't have minded if he did—

*Yes, she would.*

"What are you doing to me?"

"A test, if you will." His voice shifted back to his own, and she pushed him away.

"Very interesting, indeed."

"Stop saying that," she snapped. The music had begun again. The guests or figments—she didn't know what—began to dance in provocative movements. "I saw him. He's here, isn't he?"

Velos shrugged. "I haven't seen him. But the night is early."

Kora glared at him. "Which are you? Are you his enemy?"

His grin was feline in nature. Mischievous. Familiar to Shade's. "What am I the god of, Miss Darling?"

"Desire." Another rush curled through her blood, and she hated that he had this type of power over her. Over anyone.

"I could have you on your knees, if I wanted to. Do you know why I don't?"

She didn't deign to answer, not wanting him to prove his point.

His mouth quirked higher and curiosity flitted in his gaze. "You are intriguing, Miss Darling. That is not something anyone can doubt." He shook his head. "If I wanted to hurt him, I'd know exactly how to do it. But I haven't."

"Then what is the meaning of all of this?"

He grazed a finger along her jaw. "What would be the fun in telling you that?"

She wanted to recoil from his touch but didn't give him the satisfaction.

"I may be the host, but I'm not the only immortal in attendance. Some of the biggest pieces are present—or are going to be." He leaned in again and whispered in her ear, "Your friend is safe, and it's best she does not become a pawn. I created the game board, and it's meant to protect you. But only if you make the right moves."

Then he was gone, along with his touch. His presence. All of him.

Kora's heart beat against her chest like hands pounding against the toubeleki. What had he meant?

"Behind you."

She whirled around at the sound of Shade's voice and

searched for him in the increasingly frenetic crowd. It was becoming more difficult to tell what was real or not. A few shimmered in and out of view. Others, more solid, glanced in her direction as they passed, and she heard their whispers.

*That's his guest of honor?*

*Oh, our god is a curious man if that's whom he chose.*

*Who is she?*

But Shade wasn't amongst them. Even as she waited for the blanket of power to adjust guests' features, she didn't find the King of the Dead.

"Over here." The words were whispered like a caress against her ear. "Kora." She followed the voice's beckoning and found, within a corner, a large potted plant that closed off an empty alcove.

With slumped shoulders, she turned, annoyed with herself, when she heard an exasperated sigh.

"Wildflower."

She looked over her shoulder and glared into the corner. "What?"

"It's me. Well—a part of me."

This time she looked around to ensure no one was watching before she slid around the plant and was met with a darkness she would recognize anywhere. "Shade?"

"I'm trying to come to you."

She reached out, brushing the darkness until her hand pressed against something solid and familiar, her fingers grazing the shape of an arm. "You're a shadow."

"There is something or someone attempting to block out my presence. This is as far as I've made it through their defenses since our brief eye contact."

She remembered that moment vividly. "You mean the moment that you were surrounded by others, laughing without a care before you disappeared?"

"It seems when we saw each other that was enough to put

into play whatever this whole evening is about. I can't get to you. At least, not beyond this form."

Kora rolled her eyes, trying to hold onto an arm that wasn't fully materialized. "Then why didn't you search for me sooner if you knew I was here?"

"I was looking for you. I only received Velos' invitation today. I didn't respond to his request, hoping to sneak in here and get you out. But my plan didn't work and Velos was prepared. Not everyone is as they should be. The masks—"

"Changes identities. I know." She sighed. At least she had one less thing to be upset with him about. "So, you didn't know about the masquerade last night?"

"No or I would have warned you not to attend. As it was, I was trying to reach you before your arrival and was thwarted at every attempt."

Kora glanced over her shoulder. The music had shifted again, and guests began to dance to the seductive tune. "I knew it was something to do with you and I, but what exactly is the meaning of all of this?"

"I don't know. Velos does enjoy his games, as do his siblings. I'm certain they are a part of this too, so be careful. The evening is just beginning."

It felt like she had been here for hours already, and it was exhausting to hear that the *fun* had only just begun. "What do you mean just beginning? Shouldn't it be coming to an end soon?"

A caress, cool to the touch since it was just shadow, but she recognized his scent. The Isles. Bergamot. Want. "Shade, you've been absent."

"I've missed you, Wildflower."

"You have a strange way of showing it."

She closed her eyes as his caress slid down her throat, holding much of the promises she missed from him during the past few weeks. "Didn't the letters explain?"

Her brow furrowed. "What letters?"

"The letters I sent."

"No." She opened her eyes, wishing she could see his face and puzzle out his expression. "I never received any letters. Not in the past month."

His touch lingered at her collarbone. "Astraea was meant to deliver them."

Kora shook her head. "Not a one."

And then his touch was gone. The darkness she stared into was just that and nothing more.

Kora leaned forward into the corner, pressing her hands against the wall, searching for any sign of him. All that remained was his lingering scent.

The caress of his shadow was like a phantom against her skin. But she had wanted more. Wanted all of him. It had been too long since he touched her. Too long since he held her.

The music shifted, pulling her out of her thoughts. There was a tinge to the violin. A longing in the cello. An evocative need in the viola. Kora peered towards the dance floor from behind the wide green leaves of the bear's breech plant. As soon as she touched the glossy leaves, stems burst out and lavender flowers bloomed from the soil. Kora pulled her hand away quickly, eyes wide. She hadn't meant to do that. A glance from her palm to the newly grown purple flowers, and the music changed again. The tempo beckoned her, and though she wasn't certain what had caused the surge of her power, she couldn't ignore the lure of the song.

The mood of the ballroom had changed once again. The light from the starlit ceiling bounced off the diamond chandeliers. Prisms of soft, dream-like light spread around the room. The orchestra's rhythm was seductive—the people dancing no longer cared who saw or even seemed aware they were in public. Desire licked the air and a heaviness in her core grew with each step.

The dancing became more provocative. Kora stayed on the outskirts, unable to decipher what was real and what wasn't. If those dancing were images or those who had chosen to stay behind. Satin seats had couples and throuples wrapped within each other's arms. Skirts were hiked up, hands twisted in hair. Kora jerked her attention from a couple who landed, wrapped up within each other's arms, onto the settee beside her. That's when she noted the double doors on the other side of the room. They were wide open to what looked like a balcony overlooking a garden. She needed air. No. What she really needed was to find the answers as to why she was here.

And, without a doubt, she would need Shade.

Kora turned around and smacked face-first into a hard chest. Kora looked up and met a gentleman's rugged smile. "Sorry, miss. You looked lost."

He had his hands clasped behind his back and exuded a prestigious air from his exquisite suit to immaculately styled hair. Even his porcelain mask shone without a smudge. Judging by his pressed attire without a wrinkle in sight, he hadn't been affected by what was going on around them. "No, I'm just looking for someone."

He gave a small bow of his head. "Maybe I could assist you. There are many someones here."

"I don't think so." There was something about him. She couldn't get a read on them, which only made her more wary. It made her question once again what was real or figments of Velos' power.

"It's no bother. Who is this individual you are searching for?" If he was bothered by the writhing bodies or the growing desire that she could almost taste, he didn't show it.

"I assure you I can handle it alone, thank you. It's my escort—he's around here somewhere."

His attention shifted back to her. "I didn't see you arrive with anyone."

She stilled, fully pausing her search for Shade to scrutinize the man in front of her. "You've been watching me?"

He leaned in and winked. "Yes. Sir Edward." He gave a full bow, staring up at her expectantly. "Miss...?"

An English *gentleman*. Or so he said. The name, the air with which he spoke—it all could be an act or a shift in character brought on by Velos' power. She wouldn't give him her name. "Miss Galanis."

"Lovely to meet you, Miss Galanis." He straightened and clasped his hands behind his back. "Now what is the name of your escort? I may know who he is."

"I doubt you do. Truly, I'm fine." She moved past him, but a gust of air caused her to pause as Shade's scent mixed within.

Sir Edward took that pause as an invitation and moved in beside her. "I don't know how you expect to find them without some help."

Kora reattempted to move around him when another scent-filled gust made her stop. Was it Shade trying to tell her something? She peered at the man. "And what did you have in mind?"

"A dance."

"How is that helpful?" She glared, taking a step back from him. She didn't trust him. But curiosity had her hesitating—was he a part of this game she'd found herself in? It seemed likely since he was the only other not falling into the seduction of the music.

"We can move freely around the room." He tilted his head, considering her. "You can see everyone. I assume your escort wouldn't be among those along the perimeter. Unless you expect them to be?"

"No." She almost snapped the word but somehow kept her tone even. "He wouldn't."

"He. And his name?"

"Mr. Galanis." She swallowed deeply.

"Your brother?"

She considered the breeze that played with her skirts. If it was Shade's shadow, then gods help her if he overheard her now. "No, my betrothed."

Sir Edward snorted. "I thought only available individuals were invited to attend this soiree?"

"True. But we aren't married yet, are we?"

"Touché." He held out his arm. "Then let us dance as friends and see if we can find your Mr. Galanis."

She wanted to say no, but the breeze told her what she needed to know as it wrapped around both her and his feet. "If we must."

"I don't want to be a burden, miss."

She took his outstretched hand and gave it a slight tug to pull him onto the dance floor.

The music took on a provocative twill almost as soon as they came together. Kora tried to stay attentive not only to those around her in search of Shade, but also her dance partner. When Sir Edward tried to pull her in close, she stepped away from him.

He led her around the dance floor with ease. His steps steady, and his posture perfection. With him this close, Kora focused her attention on him.

Power radiated through her fingertips and up her arm. A god. Which one, though? "What is it you do, Sir Edward?"

"I'm in the business of relationship building. Hard work, that is."

"What is it exactly?"

He twirled her around then pulled her back and gazed into her eyes. "Would you like to find out?"

She knew the answer should be no. But intrigue and curiosity settled in her chest. "Yes."

"Close your eyes."

On their own, her eyes drifted closed. He pulled her against the hard planes of his chest. "Listen to the music," he whispered against her ear. "Feel it."

The music dipped then paused. And he did too. His hand splayed on her bare back. The hand he held, he rested it flat against this chest where she could feel his heart. The frantic beat had her pulling her hand away, but he placed his palm over her hand, holding it there. When the tempo of the music shifted to something slow and haunting, he dipped her in a low arc during a long note. She was upright as the note came to an end and then they were moving. Her feet followed his lead as she kept her eyes closed, allowing him to guide them through the space as the tempo picked up. Her breath heightened at the ferocity in which they moved, and when the music slowed, he did too.

"Did you feel that?"

She opened her eyes and stared at him as he slowed their steps to a gentle sway, until they were barely moving at all. "Felt what?"

"The rush. The need."

"I need Mr. Galanis," she said with a ragged breath. Even if she had felt the music, it wasn't her dance partner she pictured. It was Shade holding her. Moving with her. "I need to find *him*."

The music curled in another long note, and he didn't miss a beat as he dipped her again until she was staring at the starry ceiling. When she was upright, it was Shade who held her in his arms.

# CHAPTER 9

"You're not him." She gasped, then pushed against him until he let her go. "You're not Velos either. Which immortal are you?"

The smirk he wore was heart-achingly familiar. "It's me. Whatever it was that you did, Wildflower, I'm here now."

She shook her head and took a step back. Everything around her was playing tricks on her. "I don't believe you."

He chuckled, then pulled her close and wrapped her arms around his neck. "I can prove it's me if I must."

"You can't. The power in this ballroom is strong, but I'll see through it eventually."

"Oh, you are certain I can't?" The Shade lookalike grazed a finger down her spine. She shuddered and instinctively arched towards him. Bergamot and citrus filled her senses. Could they replicate his scent too?

He brushed his mouth against the curve of her ear. "This place plays with your mind. You can't trust anything you see right now." He held her possessively—one hand at her waist, the other grazing circles on her exposed back. "There's a spot you like. A touch that gets you every time."

At the caress of his words, the seduction of a voice she would recognize anywhere, she stepped in closer, her eyes fluttering closed. Her breath hitched.

His grip tightened on her waist. "Do you know me, Starlight?" His lips trailed to her neck. He breathed against her skin, inhaled. And she bared her throat to him, shivering as his teeth grazed her clavicle.

She gasped. "Shade." He grinned, then nipped. The pain was just enough to clear her mind, before clouding it with desire. For him. "It's you."

"That it is." He kissed the tender spot where he had bit her.

"I was just dancing with another." She wanted to move in closer. To have his mouth on hers. His touch was so familiar in comparison to the other god.

His expression darkened. "I'm aware."

"Who was that?"

"The God of Lust, Thélo. I was able to return just as he dipped you the first time. I couldn't move or speak—was forced to watch you dance with him."

So, the Triad was involved, not just Velos. And the reason they were here had to do with them as a couple. Did they not want them to be together? "They are testing us."

"They are." A ragged breath escaped him as he took in their surroundings. "Come, we should try to see if we can get out of here."

They moved through the crowd, sidestepping the carnal desires being played out throughout the room. "This isn't fair. All of them are spelled and don't know what they are doing nor with whom."

"Many of those who remain are illusions."

"Are you certain?" She nearly reached out to touch someone but stopped herself. "It was terrifying how so many left. They looked like the undead. Ariana was among them."

"I saw—well, the shadow version of me saw a part of it. I was trying to break free. The only ones remaining are acolytes of the Triad, but everyone else left. It seems upon their return, the Triad has taken up old practices with fervor. Like I said, be wary and don't trust anything you see."

"And I'm supposed to believe that you're here with me?" The real question she should ask was for how long. Was believing him all it would take for them to leave? It seemed unlikely.

He came to a stop and turned to face her, ignoring those around them. "Some trust is going to have to come from your instincts. Do you trust that I'm here with you now?"

Kora thought about Nanny's words of wisdom. Even with her frustration at Shade's recent absence, her mind and heart agreed that it was Shade with her now. "I trust you."

He kissed her forehead. "Good. I trust you too."

"I just hope that whatever this evening is meant to be about is over soon and Velos didn't lie when he told me Ariana was sent home. Especially so that all these other people can go home too."

Shade led her through the crowd, keeping her close to him. "He isn't a liar. Even within his games his word is bond. If he sent her home, you can be confident that is where she is. As for the others remaining, they are here by choice and choice alone. The Triad were popular before they were pulled from the world. Velos wouldn't allow anything untoward to those unconsenting."

Out of the corner of her eye, she spotted people in the midst of tearing each other's clothes off and diverted her attention away. Considering the potential consequences that came from sexual endeavors, she wondered to what extent they were prepared. "Do they have the power to stop reproduction?"

Shade glanced around and then pointed to the half-drunk wine glasses scattered about the room. "Yes. Did you drink tonight?"

She thought about it and shook her head. At one point, she almost had but had deposited the glass somewhere without a sip.

He scooped up a glass as they passed an abandoned serving tray. "You might want this. Unless..."

Her cheeks pinked as he handed off the wine, then took

her other hand and dragged her through the room, the glass still in hand and with its contents sloshing onto her fingers. "You are making assumptions. I'm not interested in being pressed against any walls tonight."

He grinned over his shoulder. "Not even by me?"

She knew her face was red, but she yanked him to a stop despite her embarrassment. His brow rose as she jabbed a finger into his chest. "You have some explaining to do." Her relief that he was here mixed with her trepidations about their current relationship status.

He had kept things from her.

"Yes, I do. Especially if you didn't receive my letters." He kissed the tip of the finger she accosted him with. "Something I'll be rectifying as soon as we are free of this place. Astraea has some questions to answer too. Until then, let's try to get you out of here."

Kora glanced down at the glass in her hand, then tipped back the wine. Just in case.

After she put the wine glass down, he continued to lead her in the direction of the double doors that led to the hallway she'd first entered through. Halfway to their destination, the doors opened and Kora grabbed Shade's arm and stopped dead in her tracks. With eyes wide, she choked on air. She tried to blink away the sight before her.

Shade turned abruptly and helped to steady her. "Kora, are you all right?"

She pointed with a shaky hand towards the last two people she expected to find. "Par...ents," Kora sputtered, looking with panic around the room of open debauchery. What would they say?

"What?"

Kora watched as Mr. and Mrs. Darling walked arm in arm with giant smiles on their faces as they took in the room. They overlooked every bit of sex and debauchery as though they were out on a leisurely stroll in town. "My parents."

Shade blanched as he glanced between her and her parents. She considered running, hiding amongst the crowd of revelers. As if the power in the room realized the severity of her conundrum, everyone moved aside to create a wide berth between Kora and her parents.

They caught sight of Kora immediately and waved. "Kora, there you are."

"Don't panic. Why aren't they panicking?" She swallowed, unconsciously straightening the creases of her dress. "Are they spelled?"

"They must not be able to see what you see." Shade glanced around the room before he cleared his throat, straightening and adjusting the mask on his face. "Do you want me to disappear?"

They were quickly approaching. Each step was a countdown to a decision she hadn't prepared for. "Do you want to?"

"Of course. But not for the reason I assume is going through your head right now."

"And what reason do you think that is?" she whispered the words, wondering if he would answer.

"I want to meet your parents. I want to be by your side, always, Wildflower. I just didn't plan for them to meet me here, and under these circumstances. I always pictured it would be if and when you were ready."

Her head jerked in his direction. "You'd thought about that?"

He was already watching her. "I've thought about every nuance and every moment with you. A future. Us. Of course I thought about meeting your parents."

She smiled. Held his gaze and nodded. She'd thought that she'd been the only one considering a future. Different scenarios of Shade coming to call on her had played in her thoughts. Mr. Darling patting his back appreciatively. Of her mother doting on him and forcing him to eat more than he could stomach. And then, at some point, maybe he'd even ask for her hand and they would spend her lifetime together. She'd continue to visit the Isles and time in the mortal world would be spent tending her garden. There would be time to expand her knowledge in botany while continuing her experiments to relieve the world should it ever suffer a famine again.

Despite his godly identity, this seemed more realistic than being bound to whatever expectations a mortal man would bestow upon her. In her mind, it was either a life with Shade or one as a spinster. There was no in between. She glanced at her parents briefly before turning fully to him. "This is not how I pictured it either. Not in a room hosted by the Triad of Love."

"Ha," Shade laughed. "They would love that name. Don't tell them...although, they probably already heard."

"What do we do?"

He moved in beside her and straightened. "I'll follow your lead. If you want to announce me as a friend or have me leave, we can do this when it is right."

Nothing about them had ever been exactly right. Their circumstances have never been normal. They had met over her brother's lifeless body and fell in love on the Isle of Waiting— amongst the dead. "Now."

He nodded, and together they turned towards her parents. This time, when Kora's gaze settled on them, she noted the third who stood behind them. Shade's hand took hers and tightened with a reassuring squeeze before he let go. When a growl of annoyance sounded from his throat, she knew he realized what she had just noticed too.

Her parents came to a stop, but Kora paid them little

attention as she pinned a glare on the immortal grinning behind them.

"Oh, hello, Little Mouse. It's been a while."

Kora glared at the King of the Sea. "Not long enough."

"I escorted your parents here. It felt appropriate, seeing that you were the guest of honor. They should be here to witness your experience."

"Wasn't that kind of Mr. Halieus." Kora's mother smiled at the Sea God. "He was so polite and kind to consider us."

"That mask is exquisitely crafted," her father added, pointing at Kora's face. "Where did you get it?"

"It was offered upon my arrival."

Mr. Darling grinned. "Well made. Impressive."

"Father. Mother. This is Mr. Galanis."

Shade bowed, keeping his attention on her parents while his hands remained gripped tightly behind his back. "It's a pleasure to meet you both."

"Pleasure has another meaning here, don't you think, brother?" Halieus's gaze darted towards Shade. "I didn't expect to find you here."

"You were the one not invited." Velos appeared on Kora's right side within a breath. "What a surprise, Halieus."

"Mr. Halieus was so kind to include us. I hope that our esteemed host doesn't mind our arrival." Kora's mother waved a fan that she fluttered open at his appearance.

"It wasn't you with whom I was regarding, Mrs. Darling." Velos sighed. "You are welcome, of course."

"Come." Halieus held his arm out to Kora's mother. "Let's get you both some refreshments."

Kora waited until her parents were retrieving a glass of wine she wasn't certain they should be drinking. "What do they see?"

Velos waved a hand in their direction. "They are going to

see the truth if you don't get them out of here soon. It's a lot of work to hold this mirage up for them."

Kora turned to Shade, only to find the spot beside her empty. She groaned out loud, other guests answering in kind, which had Kora rubbing a hand over her blushed face. "Send my parents home safely please." She crossed her arms, staring at the insufferable immortal. "You owe me for all of this."

Velos shook his head. "I can't. I don't have power over those who are not guests."

She considered her options. Would her parents willingly leave? She could lure them towards the exit. The first thing she needed to do was get them away from the Sea King. "Then get Halieus out of here. I'll take care of my parents."

"Once again, he's not a guest. My hands are tied." He held them both up in mock surrender.

Many words crossed her mind, all of them unladylike to say aloud. Normally she wouldn't care, but with her current luck her mother would overhear and scold her. "Fine. I'll do it myself." Fists formed at her side, she turned towards her parents before rounding on Velos again. "Where do you keep sending Shade?"

"I wouldn't worry about him—he'll be back when he can. I don't have control of all the pieces here. There are many figures within this room."

"Honesty. How refreshing." Kora rolled her eyes. This wasn't the first time she'd dealt with difficult immortals. A year ago, this may have seemed an impossible task. Hells, even six months ago. But she'd taken on not only Shade, but the King of the Gods as well. Somehow she'd find a way to get her parents out of here.

"Shade is capable, Kora. I think you are already aware of that."

"I do. So, then this is about me?"

He smirked. And she hadn't wanted to slap someone so

much before in her life. Well—never mind that. Halieus deserved a second one right about now.

"I can tell you this and only this—the reason Halieus arrived the way he did was because he sensed you were winning. Some of us are cheering you on."

Winning? Well, that was a good sign even if she didn't know what she was competing for and if she even wanted the prize. "I've dealt with him before, and he also lost that round."

Velos laughed. "I like you. You have ten minutes or your parents are about to get a rude awakening, and I won't be able to let them out. They will become a part of this game."

"At least, if they are a part of the game, you can let them out right?"

He shook his head. "I don't think you will want to explain to them what is happening or how Shade is involved. I do not control what desires others fall into, only give them the opportunity to use it. That is all up to them. The illusions may alter their reality, but our acolytes still have their own choices to make and if you haven't noticed they are hells bent on having fun tonight."

She glared at him and his lack of logic. "You sent Ariana and the others away. There must be loopholes."

"That was before the game had officially begun. We let you get your bearings upon your arrival, but this is only the beginning. You may have succeeded in the first trial, but there are different levels to these escapades."

Kora sighed. She knew it was beyond hope to think that this evening would come to an end that easily.

"Oh, and time is running out before the next trial begins."

She turned on her heels, unwilling to waste any more time before coming to an abrupt stop. Her parents were gone.

# CHAPTER 10

SHE SEARCHED the crowd of revelers, combing through bodies tangled together, and around groups piled on the floor in positions Kora refused to attempt to decipher whose limb belonged to whom.

Her parents were nowhere to be seen. And neither was Halieus. Ten minutes suddenly seemed impossible.

She nearly tripped on an entangled couple when a thought hit her—could she leave with them? Or, if she left, would the game end?

There were some things she was willing to do to put an end to this, but leaving her parents behind wasn't one of them.

The doors to the garden and outside balcony were open and she hadn't been out there yet. She headed outside and the chilled evening air hit her skin, jarring her for a moment. Until now, she hadn't realized how warm she had been. A trail of perspiration cooled her back at the sudden shift in temperature. It had turned unusually cold for a summer evening. Even if it was early in the season, it had her wishing for a coat. She found a marble railed balcony overlooking a small olive tree orchard. Bushes of thick bougainvillea with pretty pink flowers grew along a tall wall that outlined the property.

Her parents were standing to the far right of the balcony railing, just out of view from the doorway. Halieus was pointing out the garden below, waving a hand dramatically at the bougainvillea. "I've heard your daughter is intrigued by plants."

"She is. How do you know her?"

"We have crossed paths once or twice." Halieus caught sight of her as she stormed their way, his aggravating gaze tracing her movements over her parents' shoulders. "Here she is now."

"It's time to go." Kora came to an abrupt stop. "Thank you for including my parents in this evening's festivities, but you are unwelcome here Mr. Halieus."

"Kora, you're being rude. If Mr. Vasilis didn't want him in attendance, don't you think he would have been certain to show him out? Not send a guest to do so."

"I have an invitation." Halieus held up one in between his fingers.

She wanted to snatch the fake invitation and tear it to bits, but she knew what her mother would say. With a saccharine smile, Kora took her mother's arm. "I apologize for my rudeness. Mother, Father, please follow me. The carriage is waiting."

"Oh, but then they will miss all of the fun." Halieus' grin lengthened.

"We wouldn't want to be rude to Mr. Vasilis," Father added.

Kora bit her lip. "I need you both to leave."

"Why?" Mrs. Darling's eyes widened.

How was she meant to force them out without revealing the truth? And why now, of all times, did they have to go back to micromanaging her life? "Because there is a gentleman who has shown interest, and I think your presence may frighten him away."

"If he cannot handle meeting us, then he is not fit for you dear." Her father's tone grew gruffer with each word.

"He's shy." Kora gave a pleading look. "And I think he's quite kind. You will really like him, and I know he will want to meet you both. Just under a less public scenario." She gave her mother a sincere smile. "It's quite overwhelming here, don't you think? There are too many expectations."

"Everyone seems cordial to me," Father grumbled as he nodded towards the ballroom where the faint sharp staccato of the orchestra could be heard. "There is music, dancing, and food just like at every other one of these events."

Her hand tightened into a fist. "Everyone has been kind, but no one else's parents are here." Partial truths were the best way to appease her stubborn father.

Mrs. Darling's eyes widened. "This is true, dear. And if Kora likes him too—"

Halieus cleared his throat. "I would also like to put my name in for consideration?"

Kora whirled around to find him grinning like a jester. "Whatever do you mean?"

"I would like to court you, Kora Darling."

Her face heated. "Mr. Halieus, I assure you that this is untoward and unnecessary."

"Kora, be kind. He has been quite polite and forthcoming."

She almost had them ready to leave. She knew it. And time was counting down by the second. There was one sure way to get all of them out, and for Halieus to disappear as well.

Kora straightened and stared him straight in the eye. "Do you know the truth of how we met, Mother?"

Halieus's brow rose.

"He tried to take advantage of me. He pushed me against a wall."

He growled, his face pinching into disgust as he stepped towards her. She lifted her chin, making herself as tall as she could. Even though she only came to his chest, she wouldn't back down. "He grabbed me by the throat."

"How dare—" Mr. Darling was between the two of them, and with a ferocity Kora didn't know her father possessed, he punched him square in the jaw, knocking Halieus' head to the side.

Her mother had Kora wrapped in her arms, staring in as much shock as Kora. "Father?"

"Leave my daughter be. You are never welcome to our home."

Halieus rubbed his jaw. "You believe your daughter's words that quickly? Don't you think—"

Mrs. Darling moved in between them, and Kora didn't know if she would survive all the evening's unexpected twists as her mother pushed Halieus hard in the chest. "We believe her. We don't know you."

Halieus stared incredulously at where Mother had touched him. His gaze shifted to Mrs. Darling, a darkness deepening in his features.

Kora waved her fingers, a smile on her lips. "Goodbye, Halieus."

He narrowed his eyes at the small space between her parents, but before he could push through them, she stepped in between to stand alongside them. United. His jaw twitched. "You know this won't be the last you see of me."

"Your brother will make certain that you never cross my path again."

"My brother? And where is he now?" Halieus curved around them, holding Kora's gaze as he stared her down. "More than once he's left you unprotected in my presence. Tell me, do you think he's capable of keeping you safe?"

Without a doubt. But she also knew one other thing. "I can protect myself." She reached for her power, felt it at the ready as it thrummed to her fingertips. The bougainvillea creaked as it shifted while her parents continued to glare at Halieus beside her. Without looking over her shoulder, she knew the branches twisted and turned until they were shaped into a rather inappropriate hand gesture. "Don't come near us again," she whispered.

With a quick glance at what she had done, he took a step, but before he could act on his anger, the plant grew in size at her back. He cursed her then turned and went inside. She desperately wanted to send out a branch to trip him, but that would be hard to explain to her parents.

Kora took their hands, keeping them from turning to see what she had done as she walked them inside. "Now, please would you two go home?"

"Dear, you were quite impressive back there."

She dragged them faster into the room as her father waggled his eyebrows at his wife. "Same to you, my dear."

A seductive lilt rose in her mother's voice. "You know, I couldn't help but notice..."

"La la la la la," Kora interrupted before they could continue that thought. She could feel the room's call of lust and desire. Knew what was happening to her parents—her time was up. "I promise the conversation can wait until the carriage."

"Kora?" There was a sense of concern in her mother's voice. "What are those people doing in the corner?"

She didn't look. Didn't want to know what her mother saw.

Velos stood at the doorway to the ballroom. He tapped the face of a pocket watch that he held up. Kora began to jog.

"Kora, slow down." Her father tugged on her arm, but she didn't slow down. The doors flung open as soon as she reached them, and she trotted down the hall, ignoring the couple pressed against the wall and their echoing moans.

It took strength she didn't know she possessed to get out with both of her parents tugging her and trying to pull her back. She ignored their words. Their pleas to stop. And when she reached the entrance to the mansion, the same gray-haired masked man stood there. He didn't ask, didn't make a comment, just opened the door—

Kora came to a jarring stop, bouncing back from an invisible impact.

She dropped her parents' hands to rub her head, looking for what she had run into and saw something shimmer.

"You have little time." Diamandis stood with the door open. "Fifteen..."

"Mother, Father—I need you to leave."

"Kora, something isn't right here."

Kora glared at the masked man. Her mouth was suddenly dry, words failing her. What was she to do?

He shrugged. "Ten." He held up his two hands, dropping one finger at a time. Slowly. Counting down the seconds.

"Will they remember?"

He tilted his head. The fourth finger falling. Six seconds left. "I can help them forget."

She glanced at her parents and turned back to him with a firm nod. "Do it."

Grabbing her mother, she gave her a brisk hug and kiss on the cheek. "I love you. Understand I'm doing this for you." Mrs. Darling fell to the ground as Kora pushed her out and winced with a small gasp of her own shock at what she'd done.

"Kora!" her father bellowed and rushed towards his wife, gasping as he leaned over her. "What did you do?"

She glanced back at Mr. Diamandis who stood with the door open. "Do it now. Send them home. Let them forget being here."

He nodded, and Kora watched as her mother eerily sat up, her attention shifted towards Mr. Darling. "Let's go home. It's too late to be out, don't you think?"

"I do."

Neither looked back towards the mansion. To Kora.

The door closed just as her parents got to their feet. Her

father's question to her mother about how they had got there in the first place were the last words she heard.

Her body shook. She had literally dragged her parents through a scandalous party and thrown her mother out the door. "They won't remember?"

"No."

"They will be home safe and sound?"

"I'll make certain of it." Mr. Diamandis had his hands folded behind his back as he surveyed her.

"Who are you?"

The man grinned. "One of the players."

Her gaze narrowed. "Which one?"

He chuckled. "It doesn't matter—yet."

Then he was gone, and Kora was left alone with her thoughts, trying to let everything settle. Halieus had come. She had only made it through part of whatever "trial" this was. She needed to get out. And she knew she would need Shade to do it.

# CHAPTER 11

As Kora walked down the hall back towards the domed ballroom, a plan began to form in her mind. She had been playing by their rules this entire time and letting the shock of each unexpected turn distract her. She had never been good at playing by her parents' rules or society's expectations. Sure, forging her own path hadn't been easy. University wasn't the dream she had hoped it to be with its limits on women studying as well as their meager access to botany studies. But that disappointment didn't mean she needed to do what was expected of her here. She'd asked a lot of questions but was waiting for the answers to come to her instead of finding them herself. There had been hints as to what she was meant to do. And without a doubt, it had to do with Shade.

She'd resisted Velos' desire when he'd tried to use it against her and was rewarded with Shade's presence. That had to mean something.

When she reached the double doors, she flung them open and made an entrance that had many pausing from whatever positions they were in to glance her way. She looked at all the manners of undress. Took in the vulnerable positions she found them all in before turning her attention to the center-pieces upon tabletops. Flowers of ivory and blood red. Bouquets with poppies and roses. Others with lavender and gardenias. Some with jasmine and chamomile. Vines of ivy hung from the edges of the dome amidst the colorful ribbons. She concentrated on the flowers first, strengthening their scent, taking the once-seductive aroma and using their relaxing properties to induce drowsiness. Pollen drifted into the air, spreading through the room. It took only a few minutes for eyes to drift closed. Those that had only been illusions paused their movements, then slowly dissipated until they no longer remained.

She'd never done this before. Never considered what her power could do. Kora had always thought of plants as a source of life. Food. To save her family and world from famine. The music halted abruptly, the orchestra slumping against their instruments or one another. As a few yawned and curled up amongst each other, she turned towards the ivy. It grew, lengthening and thickening until there was a wall of green leaves circling the perimeter, hiding the sleeping guests from view. She knew it couldn't last forever since there was only so much pollen, but that was all the time she would need to win this game she had found herself playing.

A slow clap had Kora turning around, and she took in the man before her. He was the one she had danced with during her last test. Sir Edward...or in truth, Thélo. "It's your turn now, isn't it?"

He grinned. "You like to surprise us, Kora. There were whispers of a mortal-turned-god."

"No." She shook her head. "I'll end that gossip right here. I'm no god."

He chuckled. "You think a mere mortal can do what you just did?"

"I could only do so because one of your kind slept with a mortal, and I got to reap the benefits of that union. That power helped save my world. Nothing more."

He considered her for a moment. "You don't know, do you?"

"Know what?" His words made her wary. She'd thought she had taken back some control. The music had stopped, the orchestra asleep on that stage—the only ones who had remained unaffected by the desire and lust that had overtaken the others. She knew they were a pivotal piece to their games. But what he was saying now...

"Your time in Nekrós is changing you."

Her throat constricted. "What?"

"Oh, I think it's time. For just a moment, you will be rewarded with the truth. You did win the first game, after all."

Shade appeared beside the man, and before Kora could collect her thoughts, he had him by the throat. "What the fuck, Thélo."

"She deserves—" Thélo choked, eyes bulging as Shade tightened his grip.

"Yes she does. I was trying to tell her before you decided to pull this shit." Shade flung him to the ground, and Kora saw the shadows inch towards the prone immortal and grab hold, pinning him down.

With Thelos currently occupied as he fought the shadows, Shade turned towards her. "Please, let me explain—" He took in the room, attention held on the wall of vines. "Did you do all of this?"

*She needed him to win this game.* A part of her told her that. The part that tried to get through her jumbled-up thoughts. "Tell me what, Shade?" Her anger was winning.

"The letter I sent you. It explained everything. Astraea was supposed to explain everything. Why I've been absent and distracted. What I was doing instead."

"Which was what?"

He walked towards her with his hands raised in submission, as though she was a violent animal prepared to attack. "I noticed it. The little bits and pieces over time. Your magic is changing, shifting."

Fists formed at her side.

"Your power is growing. Adapting to you and the world. Your time in Nekrós seems to exasperate it."

"You're saying a lot of words to go around the one important thing you've left unsaid."

He swallowed, stopping an arm's length away from her. "You're becoming immortal."

Air lodged in her throat. She couldn't swallow. Move. She was ensnared by his gaze. The words were like a noose around her neck.

"I'm so sorry, Kora. This is not what I wanted for you. If I had known, I would have warned you sooner. I would have told you that day I almost lost you. It had never crossed my mind that by feeding you those seeds, this would be the consequence. I had just wanted to save you."

"And then die?" She gasped out the words. "That was your plan for us?" Tears welled in her eyes. "That we would have an end? You wouldn't be tied to me forever if I stayed mortal." Because that was the part that hurt the most. Not that he didn't tell her in person, nor that she heard first from someone else.

The Isles had become a second home to her, but that wouldn't make it any less difficult when it was her turn to enter as one of the souls. Astraea had visited every month to speak about her power and had her give demonstrations upon each of her visits to the Isles. Not once had she hinted that Kora's ability was becoming more. Shade hadn't either, even as he'd stood by her side and seen what she could do. The plants she grew. The tree on Anamoní that she had brought back to life. Not only had they kept the truth from her, but it seemed Shade hadn't even considered that she might want the opportunity to be with him forever.

"I meant it when I said you were worth fighting for. You are my choice. Always." He reached for her, but before she could decide if she wanted to go to him or not, he was gone.

A sob wracked her chest, and she fell to her knees.

Teardrops fell to the ground between her shaky hands as

she pressed them into the marble with her fingers splayed out. Her stomach twisted and that spot in her chest ached tenfold. The building rumbled.

"Kora." She recognized Velos' voice and heard the warning in the sound of her name. Her gaze snapped up. He had been moving towards her, but as soon as their eyes met, he froze in place. "Your magic is volatile this way."

"Not magic." She felt it thrum within her. "Power." She lifted her hands, sitting back on her heels to stare at them. The mansion stopped shaking.

"What are you angry about right now? Many would kill for the chance of immortality."

"I know the heartache that comes with it."

"Hm." Velos considered her.

Monos. Shade's true name—alone.

When she looked up, Velos was gone. The green vines draped the floor, and some had browned and dried. The flowers on the tables were dead. She cursed the mask, unable to wipe the tears from her cheeks. She'd done this. Had gone too far and killed the plants.

Kora got to her feet. "Let's get this over with," she spoke to the God of Lust who had been watching her quizzically from his seated position on the ground, the shadows gone.

The guests began to stir as the fragrance that kept them drowsy dissipated.

As she was considering bringing the flowers back to life, they disappeared. Within a blink, roses in shades of deep red and merlot were on the tables in their place. Kora sighed, no longer interested in using her power anyway.

People parted the ivy, stepping back onto the dance floor. A few vines fell and crumbled on impact. The orchestra rubbed their eyes, adjusting their instruments and the illusions began to reappear.

Thélo disappeared from the dance floor and reappeared

upon the stage. With a grin, he slipped his hands in the pockets of his trousers and watched her. The guests and musicians didn't miss a beat—as if they hadn't just been unconscious a moment before. The music picked back up again on the note they had stopped. Dancers began to find partners again. Acolytes found each other in dark corners. It was as if Kora hadn't done anything at all.

Only she and Thélo stood still, staring at each other while the others began to move to the music. Writhe to it. Thélo's power licked at her. A swirl that she could taste and sense but didn't affect her. He took a step towards her and instinct had her straightening, defiance etching her expression. He stopped with an arm's length between them. She wiped her face with the back of her hand.

"You feel it, don't you?"

"It's not affecting me." Her hands formed into fists, nails biting little moons into her palms.

His grin turned feral. "Not yet."

Then a lick of that power stroked her skin. She nearly buckled at the sudden need that coursed through her and had her pressing her legs together for friction. "I won't hold back like my brother did."

She bit back the moan of desperation as he pulled back his power with a flick of his wrist. A flourish she doubted he needed to do. "Why are you doing this?"

"We have our reason." He considered her. "Monos made a mistake. He kept things from you. You're becoming a god."

Why that reality didn't frighten her was something to dissect and consider later, but she couldn't let go of Shade's reaction to the truth. He wasn't happy about the alternative to her death. Earlier, he had mentioned thinking about the future—their future. Pretty words and nothing more. Her heart ached at that reality. "It seems that way, yes."

"I'll give you a chance. You can leave now. This evening will be over."

"Or?"

"Or stay here and find out what lust really means. I doubt you've felt its full effect before."

"And if I leave?"

"Why must there be anything untoward?"

She considered the immortal before her. He was the epitome of handsome. The word could be defined by his physique and features. His appearance shared many similarities to Shade, and she wondered whether each individual who looked upon him saw him differently depending on their own definition of attractiveness. Even so, she knew the truth—he wasn't the one she wanted. Even when she was hurt by him, she would always want Shade. "There is always a give and take. None of you just give."

His eyes darkened. "We don't give?" Thélo leaned in, his mouth taut. "That is all we do. Every feeling. Every life. If we didn't give, then why did your world suffer for nearly fifty years? Why did famine spread?"

She paused, taken aback by his words. She couldn't deny his claims were true. However, it wasn't the whole of the truth. "I wouldn't be here if there wasn't something you wanted. If I chose to walk out the door, I doubt that there wouldn't be repercussions."

His mouth twisted. Another rush of lust curled through her. Suddenly her dress itched, warmth settled low in her belly with a pressure at her core. Her breasts felt heavy, and her body thrummed with a want that could only be sated by touch. Her eyes closed, and she fell to her knees with her arms wrapped around her waist.

"Please," she moaned.

"What is it you want, Kora?"

"Stop it."

His laugh was melodious. Tempting. "Are you going to leave?"

She didn't want to. Instead, she wanted to be held and relieved from this overwhelming desperation. But there was a reason she was here, and he didn't have to say it for her to know. "I'm not leaving Shade."

"I'll free him if you leave."

"At what cost?" She groaned again at the thought of him appearing now. He'd alleviate this need within her—

She was mad at him, she reminded herself. She knew there was a reason for all of this. The immortals had gone through a lot of trouble, and there was no way that she could walk out without consequences. Even if they weren't her own, she knew either she or Shade would not leave unscathed.

"Only one way to find out."

There was something she could do—she could run.

So, she did. To escape Thélo.

She pushed past whoever ended up in her path, uncaring as she dodged through the dancers. There had been a moment when someone had reached for her and instinct pulled her towards them. She'd never felt like this before, and it was so maddening how close she was to unraveling. Distance had to be the key. And as much as she wanted to be touched, to come undone, there was only one being she trusted with her body.

Thélo laughed, the sound following her as she rushed up the stairs to the balcony that overlooked the domed room. On the second floor, she began to open doors, peering within for other guests. Currently, she didn't trust herself near anyone else.

More than once, she heard others who had fallen to their lust. One screamed at her intrusion, but most weren't even aware of her as she had appeared in the doorway, too involved with their partner or partners to care. At the fifth door, she walked into silence.

Hands grabbed her, pulling her close to them. The piercing blackness left her unaware of who they were. Her body was alight at the thought of finding release, but a small part of mind unaffected by lust's power told her to escape.

"Stay," someone whispered in her ear, rubbing against her peaked nipples. Another reached for her hips. Her body reacted, relaxing into the touch. A third—or, at least, she could only assume there were three—breathed against her neck causing shivers of pleasure down her spine. "You smell like sex."

"You need this," another groaned.

She gasped as a mouth trailed across her chest, following the V of her dress. Her skin felt on fire as the individual's beard scratched her sensitive skin.

This was not Shade. And she needed to get out now.

# CHAPTER 12

SHE TRIED to tear her limbs from their grips. Pulled and yanked.

"You know this is what you want. Why are you fighting it?"

Kora freed her left hand, her other arm still grasped, and her leg pinned against the wall. "You're not him," she growled. "Leave me alone."

Stumbling as they suddenly let go, the figures disappeared into the darkness of the room. She turned sharply, using her hands to search for the doorknob and twisted it open. When she shut it behind her, she pressed her back against the door, attempting to catch her breath in the relative safety of the dimly lit hallway.

Thélo's power wasn't as strong now, but a lingering ache had settled in her core. Like an itch she couldn't scratch, she concentrated on escaping that want. She didn't know how to pass this test. How long could she resist lust?

Pausing, she considered whether it was truly a matter of resisting it, or if there was another way to succeed.

"Kora?" The voice came from the steps. "This is your last chance. Do you choose to leave?"

She needed a moment to think. A chance to consider her options. To figure out how leaving could negatively affect her. There had to be a reason for all of this. She knew that. But what was it? And maybe that was the truth of the game. To uncover the why.

"I'll find you. You can't hide for long."

Kora trotted on silent steps down the carpeted hall and came to the second to last door. Two more chances to hide. If one could truly hide from lust.

She clicked open the door as quietly as she could and closed it just as carefully behind her before examining the room. Two candles were settled on an otherwise bare desk in the center. A sofa—thankfully empty—was positioned against the one wall that wasn't shelved with books, under two arched windows. Light arched off something on the shelf, nestled between a book and a decorative vase. This was the first room she saw that held knickknacks or any sign of ownership. Kora made her way across the room to find a music box with a couple dancing on top that glistened in gold and refracted the candlelight around the cozy space.

She traced the outline of the couple, and she started as they turned at her touch with a few notes of a song jarring her. She snapped her hand back and whirled at a sudden click, her heart pounding as the door handle slowly turned. She pulled in a lung full of air to hold her breath. But as the door opened and a figure emerged, air escaped her.

His gaze was already piercing hers as he closed the door behind him. "Hello, Wildflower."

Those lingering effects she had been trying to bury were brought to life. Want. Desire. Lust...

All by that gravely way he said her nickname. "Shade," she whispered it like a question.

"Do I need to prove it's me again?" He crossed the room slowly, his movements predatory.

"No."

He stopped at the desk, his gaze lingering on each curve and dip of her body. That look alone left a trail of heat she couldn't ignore. "I don't think I've told you just how beautiful you make that dress. Even if it's from Velos, no one could make it look as gorgeous as you do."

She ignored the compliment. "You didn't tell me." Kora held up a hand as he opened his mouth. She needed to get this out and pretty words weren't going to stop her. "Even if you sent letters, that wasn't fair. It should have come directly from you." Her body didn't want to fight with him. Her skin ached for his touch. But her mind told her she needed answers. Deserved them.

"I didn't mean to hurt you and for that I'm sorry. I wanted to have found out all the answers and information I could before I spoke to you. It wasn't the proper way to deal with this issue."

*Issue.* She didn't like that word. "I don't need you to protect me. Not like that."

His gaze darted down her body and pinned on the hand she had pressed against her stomach. "I know."

She gasped as his eyes traced every rise and fall of her chest. His hands gripped the back of the desk chair as if it was the only thing restraining him. Was Thélo's power affecting him too?

"Then why did you do it?" *Why don't you want me to live forever?*

"If something like this was to happen, I wanted it to be your choice. Not something I forced upon you. It was all my fault."

Kora swallowed as he took a step closer, and he immediately stopped.

She held his gaze. "I don't blame you for this."

"I fed you the seeds. I didn't warn you of the consequences."

"Did you know this was an alternative?"

He was silent. Stared.

"Did you know?"

Shade held her gaze. "I didn't know. But I also didn't not know. There were too many unknown variables."

He took another step and she stiffened, pressing back against the bookcase. Shade froze again. "Do you fear me, Wildflower?"

"No."

"Then why are you shivering?"

She hadn't even realized she was. Not with the heat of his gaze scorching her. "It won't stop."

"What won't stop?" he asked, his voice a rumble that caressed her skin as though he was at the crook of her neck.

"This feeling. His power."

"Thélo?"

She nodded, uncertain if she could speak.

"I can help with that, if you wish."

"No." She shook her head violently. "Then they win."

"What do you mean?" He moved slowly towards her, and she couldn't deny that every part of her wanted him to move faster.

"I mean that if I give in, that means they won."

His features softened. "What has this whole evening been about, Kora?"

Her heartbeat accelerated against her ribs. "Us."

He nodded.

"But I don't know what. Do you?"

"Only guesses." He moved closer and this time she didn't stop him.

She pinched her eyes closed against the onslaught of want and need to piece together her own assumptions.

His knuckles brushed against the column of her throat and she gasped. "They said you passed the first test."

"Yes. That was before I even knew I was a part of whatever games this is."

"Correct. And what did you do?" His breath curled against her cheek as he whispered in her ear.

"Pushed away Velos." And then Shade appeared. Took his place. She had chosen him over another.

She considered the timeline of events. "You disappeared."

"Not by choice. I would have been by your side this entire evening if they had allowed it. I've been pulled away from you each and every time. My power isn't as strong in the mortal world and right now, I've hated that more than anything."

"So, you're my reward?"

He nodded. "I think so."

If that's true... "Why do this? Am I proving myself to be worthy of you?"

"If anyone needs to prove their worthiness, it's me." His lips grazed her neck. "Let me help you now."

She arched into him as his hand skated over the exposed skin of her arm, until his fingers intertwined with hers and he lifted her arm up, pinning it against the bookcase. Kora's breathing heightened as his other hand grabbed hold of her thigh, moving the slit of her dress aside. He pulled up gently, until he was nestled between her with a leg wrapped around his waist. She moved against him, tugging him closer, searching for friction.

He growled against her throat, kissing the sensitive spot between her neck and collar bone.

"Shade," she whispered into the air. "Please."

His lips found hers, silencing her pleas. He kissed her with ravenous need, as though he had been the one tested by Thélo's power. His fingers dug into her thigh as he positioned himself at the apex of her center. Pressed into her. She groaned against his mouth. She didn't feel the bookcase at her back. Was barely aware of any discomfort. His tongue slid between her lips, and she met his kiss in kind. Consumed him. The taste and feel. It only left her wanting more.

She almost pulled away to beg him for release, but he must have already known. He hoisted her other leg around his waist, holding her against him while continuing to kiss her with fervor as he carried her to the sofa. Shade dropped her unceremoniously onto the soft seat. She stared up at him in awe as he tossed his coat aside and rolled up the sleeves of his shirt to his elbows. Kora licked her lips as darkness and flickering candlelight played with his features—enhancing and mystifying him all at once. Her legs widened on instinct as he came to his knees before her, settling himself in that spot she created.

He leaned forward, lips pressing into her to kiss her fully. Slowly, he pulled back and lowered further between her legs. Her eyes widened, uncertain what to do. Shade grinned up at her. "I'm going to take care of you, Wildflower. Do you trust me?"

She nodded.

"I'm going to need to hear you say it."

Her heart hammered against her chest. Each beat a resounding yes.

Her head? It pleaded for his touch. To take whatever he was offering her.

She listened to them both. "I trust you, Shade."

"I'm glad to hear that." He lifted the fabric of her dress, stared at her undergarments as though she were a gift to be unwrapped. "I'm yours, Kora." He met her eyes as he shifted her underwear aside with gentle fingers. "If you ever need or want me to stop, all you have to do is say so."

His hand pressed against the sensitive apex of her thighs. She groaned at just that hint of touch. "Don't stop."

His grin was filled with mischievous intent. "That's my girl."

Then he dipped his head and pressed a kiss to that bundle of nerves. She arched into him, her eyes closing at the sensation his touch elicited.

"Shade—" She gasped as his tongue moved in a languid slide at her center.

"Yes?" He pulled back ever so slightly, and she looked down to meet his gaze.

"That..." Words failed her. They had been intimate before, and maybe it was Thélo's power but this was...something new.

"Watch, Kora."

Her eyes widened at his request.

"Watch me take you apart and give you what you need."

He pressed his mouth to her again and consumed her. As though she was his salvation, he worshipped between her legs. Each touch, each lick, the movement of his mouth against her brought her closer and closer to that precipice. And every time she was on the edge, he slowed just a little. Played with her.

Until she was begging, her fingers twisted in his hair, pressing his mouth firmly against her.

She cried out as she came undone, her body shuddering against him with her thighs pressing against his ears.

As she came down from the sensation, he pressed a gentle kiss to the inside of her thigh. With no desire to move, her entire body relaxed against the chair. Shade sat up and leaned in to kiss her cheek, but she turned her mouth to his, tasting herself on him. He kissed her deeply. Fully.

"Shade—" she gasped, trying to speak when the world felt like it was moving through molasses. Complete contentment replaced the sheer need that had consumed her moments before.

"Feeling better, Wildflower?"

Kora closed her eyes, laid her head back against the sofa and could only nod.

He chuckled as he righted her underwear, then fixed her skirt. "This might not be the right time, but I've tried to make it a perfect moment so many times before and failed."

She peeked an eye open, watching him. When she noted his fidgeting hands, she sat up and gave him her full attention. "What is it?"

He bit his lip. She'd never seen him so nervous and suddenly she was back to wondering if there had been more to his silence on her immortality. "I..." His gaze hardened. "Fu—"

Then he was gone. Again. And she cursed as loudly she could into the empty room.

# CHAPTER 13

## SHADE

"—UCK!" Shade cursed as he was plopped into the room for an unfathomable number of times that night.

But this time as he rushed to his feet from where he'd been sprawled on the floor, he wasn't alone. He whirled around to find Velos and Thélo standing together at the desk, considering him.

His power lashed out, shadows twisted and grabbed hold of their torsos, pinning their arms to their sides and curving around their legs to hold them in place. "You have a lot of explaining to do."

Velos tilted his head and with a sneer, the shadows dispersed. Thélo chuckled, his arms crossed over his chest, muscles rippling. He was the one Shade was most annoyed with. "You're playing with mortals. This is shit and you know it."

"For fifty years you ruined their lives by ignoring your purpose," Thélo snapped. "Don't try to play their hero just because you've gone and fallen for one of them."

"Was one." As usual Velos was pure control and calculation. "She isn't anymore. He's always had a soft spot for the living, though."

Fists formed at Shade's side. "All of this was one of the positives of your absence these past years. Even if they couldn't figure out how to survive, at least they weren't under your manipulations."

Velos chuckled.

Shade's power coursed through him at the sound. He lunged, grabbing Velos by the lapels of his suit and twisting his hands into the fabric. Thélo moved towards him but with a raised hand from Velos, he stopped. "Let her out." Shade was inches from the immortal's face. "Now. I won't ask again."

"I can't." Velos' brows rose. "She's on the last test."

"This is your game board. You can do anything you want."

He shook his head. "No. This portion is not mine."

"Whose is it?" Shade roared. There were two options: love or heartbreak.

Thélo laughed. "She's made it this far. You shouldn't be concerned, Monos."

He cringed at his true name. Hated it for all its meaning. "It's Shade now."

"We know." Velos sighed. "We want it to stay that way."

Shade let go of Velos' coat and pushed him away. "This was some ploy to have her prove herself? Fuck you. If anyone needs to—"

"It's you?" Velos adjusted his coat and brushed the sleeves off as though Shade's touch had soiled it. "We know. That's why this is about both of you. We don't know her, and we thought we knew you. She brought you back, but we need to know if she will stick around. Even when you're messing up. Especially since you keep digging yourself into little holes."

He swallowed and considered the two gods before him. "I'm trying to be worthy of her without your involvement. Now let me go to her and help her out of this. And none of you will ever interfere in either of our affairs ever again."

"We can't change things." Thélo's jaw worked. He might have followed his brother's orders, but he didn't like being told what to do by anyone else. "And you aren't necessary. Yet. There is nothing you can do here. So, sit back and wait your turn."

Darkness played at his edges. He could feel it beckoning,

calling for him to wield. But he was in the mortal world and there was little he could do here. "What happens if I just tear you two apart and get her out of here?"

They both chuckled and the sound grated on Shade's last nerve.

Velos sighed, assessing him. "Outside the doors right now are your enemies, Shade. They want her. Tonight was about appeasing those who want to call you an ally, but it was also to keep your enemies at bay."

Shade's shoulders drew back, his anger only growing. "If they touch her—"

"They won't." Thélo crossed his arms. "At least not tonight. We couldn't make the same promise for you, though."

Kora would succeed. Of that he had no doubt. Then he'd get her out of here and be certain to protect her at all costs. If she'd still have him, there was a future awaiting them.

He ran a hand through his hair. "It's Áxios who remains, isn't it?"

"You should be glad it is them and not Apóle. She came, of course. But we told her we would only call if necessary."

"So far, we haven't considered that alternative—don't make us change our mind."

Apóle wasn't one of the Triad, but a sibling that was as alone as Shade had been. She found comfort in frivolous items instead of people. Named for heartbreak, she didn't want to continuously deal with the pain of mortals.

Shade considered what Kora's last test would be. A dance for desire. Seduction for lust. Love... Áxios was benevolent and smart. A dangerous combination when love was involved. They took their role very seriously. True love wasn't a game to them.

Velos' brow rose as Shade's power stuttered to life and the

darkness edged around him, forming into his shadow. "Those are just parlor tricks here. Besides, this is for your own good as much as hers. We can't have a repeat of the past. Theileus may believe all is well, but if he ever fears your power, he might cordon you off to Nekrós again."

"Fears me?" Shade had never wanted to challenge his brother, but he wouldn't be surprised if Theileus believed otherwise. He was controlling at the worst of times.

His brother had dropped him off in the Isles of the Dead and thought he'd be content there amongst the souls that were delivered to their eternal rest—or damnation.

Soon after, Theileus and Halieus had slowly disappeared. Pulled away from him. Abandoned him to a post that he'd never asked for. He'd done as he was told until he couldn't take it anymore. He'd broken away, and then over time discovered he'd also broken the world. Theileus had called the gods away from the mortal world, unable to control his subjects whilst he filled in for Shade's absence.

"Of course." Velos took a seat at one of the overstuffed chairs near the burning fire. "Your power is in the dead. A requirement for life. Theileus has much to fear."

Shade glanced to his left at the shadow figure that stood beside him. The shadow had been useful to talk to Kora on his behalf. A way to show her he was trying to help her. A perfect alternative as he'd tried to unravel the Triad's plans. But the shadow figure was also a distraction. Each test. Each moment she'd found him. It was all a distraction from who he really was. What he could do.

"That's an interesting fact to consider."

"What is?" Thélo grumbled.

"All this power you speak of." He glanced up at them through his lashes. Stared at them, his chin tucked to his chest. "Sometimes I forget what I'm capable of."

Then he snapped. Darkness formed more figures of shadows until the room was filled with them. This time when the brothers tried to escape, they couldn't do anything but scream.

# CHAPTER 14

WHEN KORA HAD EXITED the study, a figure had been standing with a hip against the railing, overlooking the ballroom below.

Silver hair hung to the shoulders of their slender build. Tight, dark silver trousers clung to slim calves, and a V-neck tunic revealed an athletic build that left little to the imagination. The mask they wore was white ceramic. It held no adornments or hint of their station.

"Who are you?" Kora swallowed deeply as she approached them.

With a tilt of their head, the name came to the tip of her tongue just as they asked, "Do you want to make a guess?"

"Áxios?" she said, naming the last member of the Triad.

They smiled. "I'm glad to know my name still precedes me. There was a time when I questioned if love was enough anymore. If it could last forever."

"It does. I know that."

Áxios laughed, the sound like a melody—not harsh nor mocking. "Not when death, the future and so many unknowns come into play. People question everything."

"And you think I am, that's why you're here? To see if I question my feelings for Shade?"

They shrugged. "It is a question, isn't it? Immortality might be your future, but does that mean anything to either of you?"

Kora shook her head. "Love doesn't end with death. Love is the reason we grieve. It's also what helps us heal. It is what helps us feel any semblance of whole once again. Because of those around us who love and allow us to lean on them."

Áxios' expression turned melancholic. "What a lovely sentiment."

"It's not just a sentiment, but a truth. I lost my brother. I miss him every day. And I love him and wouldn't trade any of the time we had—good or bad."

Áxios' brow rose, a smile tilting at the corner of their mouth. "Then this final challenge should be easy for you."

"Proving that love exists through pain and loss wasn't enough?" Kora asked hopefully.

"There are pretty words, and then there is proving it. Love isn't just words, it's action."

"And what is it you want me to do?"

"There are some unresolved things between the two of you. Find him. If he loves you and you love him, it should be easy. You must decide if he's worth it."

"And if he's not?" There had been a lot of talk about death, and although Kora may be becoming immortal, she didn't believe the process was complete enough that a god couldn't take her life if they so choose.

"Then you walk out this door. This was never about life or death, Kora," they said as if reading her mind. "In fact, we are who life stems from. Love, desire, lust...those are all things needed to create life. So, in fact, death and life need us to spur the circle. Or, as was proven with Monos' absence, there isn't much left to continue forward."

"What was it about then? Why put me—us—through all of this?"

"We can't have the past repeat itself."

The famine. Their imprisonment. They wanted to know if she was a liability or if she could control him. "I'm not his keeper."

"No, you're not. But you're our only chance right now."

Áxios grinned. "And others are going to come for you. The question is if you'll be ready for them. Some don't play as nice as we do."

"If you think this was nice, I can't imagine what others have planned." She considered them and if there was any other information she could gain before she began. "Why did you choose this type of trial?"

"As Velos told you, there are many who are rooting for you, but are uncertain and have many questions—just as you do. We offered to be the ones to test your relationship." They smiled. "If you succeed, many will be thrilled. If you don't..."

She didn't need them to finish that sentence. Not if tonight was any hint as to what could come. "And Haelieus hadn't been a part of the game?"

"There are some things I cannot say."

It seemed that was all she was going to get from the deity. Kora rested her hands on the railing and looked below and gasped. "What in the hells is this?"

Áxios peered down and their smile grew. "I didn't say it would be easy to find him."

Below them was a sea of Shades. Every single individual looked exactly like him. Wore his face. The same suit, the same shoes. When she had gasped, they had all looked up at her in unison.

At least they had stopped fornicating... She didn't know how she would feel about watching Shade make love to himself—real or not. The ones who had once been undressed were now clothed. The music had stopped too and a silence filled the room that heightened her sense of unease along with the blank way they stared at her.

"Your control over living beings is despicable."

They shrugged. "They chose their gods."

Kora turned to face them, her gaze hardening. "They should choose better."

"Nothing is better than true love." They smiled. "Let's see if you find out the truth of that."

Kora had found Shade before, and she had no doubt she'd find him again. There was no one she knew better. All she would need to do was follow her heart and her mind. They would lead her where she needed to be.

"He is here somewhere." Áxios straightened, sweeping locks of silver hair behind their shoulder. "And because we have known that you've found him here before under similar circumstances, this time you will lose your sense of smell."

With those words, all scent vanished. Kora touched the tip of her nose, not realizing how much scent had surrounded her prior to its absence. There was no longer the sweet sugary scent of the flowers. The earthy scent of their roots.

"Or sensation of touch."

Kora inhaled deeply as she no longer felt the fabric draped over her body. She looked down to be certain she was still wearing clothes. The ground was the only thing she was aware of, but what would the feeling at the bottom of her feet do for her?

"Or sound." A pop, and then nothing could be heard. She reached for her ears, rubbing them, hoping to bring back something.

*I'd take your eyesight, but that doesn't help our cause.* Their voice was thick in her head, causing her to jump in surprise. They smiled at her reaction and reached up and brushed a finger to her lips. *And no voice.*

She opened her mouth, but even if she could hear, she knew she didn't produce any sound. Resolve settled over her. Her senses would return. All she had to do was find Shade.

They turned Kora's body in the direction of the stairs and leaned towards her ear.

*Good luck.*

She took each step one by one, searching the crowd for the

real him. *He will come to me.* She thought the words in her mind.

*You don't think I already considered that?*

Kora had her suspicions, but at least that was one option to cross off her list. He'd spoken to her as a shadow. She'd recognized his scent. The second time, it had been by his touch. Although...a very specific touch. If he didn't elicit the same reaction as before, how would she know it was him?

*Your heart and your mind may be at war at times but use both.* Nanny's words echoed in her thoughts. It felt like a lifetime ago that she'd said them. Many times tonight, she'd checked in with both. This next time would be the same.

As she reached the ballroom, many of the Shade doppelgängers continued their conversations. Some watched her with the same attention she gave them. None moved in her direction. None called for her. Searched for her. The last bit of hope that he'd somehow overcome whatever control they had over him disappeared. This was all on her to solve.

*Find the man she loved.*

She said the words to herself over and over. Her heart beat faster. She didn't have her senses to rely upon, but when she saw him, she would know the truth. There were little nuances that made him who he was. She was certain that even as each figure moved aside and others observed her with those same blank expressions, one would stand out.

The immortal who kept things from her.

Her mind jumbled.

The one who didn't want to spend eternity with her.

A lifetime was one thing. Eternity was never ending. Should she blame him if he didn't want eternity with her? Did she want that with him?

*Yes.* Her heart picked up once more at the thought.

But that wasn't something she would ever force on

another. She deserved to know the truth though and to know if she had given her heart to the right man.

She stopped in the middle of the dance floor and stared up at the orchestra who also wore Shade's face. "I'd never force him to choose me." She couldn't hear the words, but others glanced at her with confused expressions. None were the real Shade.

The real Shade wouldn't force such a choice onto her.

Everything he's worked for has always been about choice. Did he worry that she wouldn't choose him? So many others had walked away from him, but in her short blip of a life in comparison to his centuries, could she blame him for questioning if she felt the same way?

When everyone else had abandoned him, how could he be certain she would stay? That thought firmed her resolve.

She had to find him. Her search became frantic as Kora pushed through the crowd, the figures a blur of copper hair and blue eyes. Eyes that didn't hold the proper amount of mischievousness to be her Shade.

He was everywhere yet nowhere.

Air whooshed out of her lungs, her body bending over at a sudden impact, but she didn't feel an ounce of pain. She frowned at the chair she had inadvertently rammed into. She was rubbing her thighs out of habit when her eyes caught the lupines that had replaced the red rose centerpieces on the tables.

Power. Life. "Find him," she tried to whisper. Nothing happened. Kora didn't feel that spread of power sing through her veins as she usually did.

Could they have blocked that part of her too?

No. It had been there even when she even tried to hold it back in her garden. She reached for that power within her, closed her eyes and breathed a slow long breath out. "Find him." All she did was mouth the words but the plants...they never responded to her voice anyway.

On an instinct that connected them, Kora opened her eyes and roots of shimmering gold appeared from her feet. At first, they branched off in every direction, searching for the best path. Some shot in different directions while others went through a few of the Shade look-a-likes. But they didn't stop there, as she knew they wouldn't—none of these imposters were him.

Another sensation caught her attention. One that went beyond touch, hearing, and smell. Knowledge. Of the immoral she loved.

Like a hand held out for her to grasp, she reached for that sensation. Her magic led her towards the stairs she had come down just moments before. Áxios stepped aside as Kora reached the landing.

A small quirk of their lips, and they gestured for Kora to lead the way.

Without wasting any time and no longer needing her magic, she jogged towards the door the tendrils had passed through and to the one she knew was waiting behind. She flung it open to find Shade standing beside the other two other members of the Triad. Velos and Thélo stood stock-still with shadow figures surrounding them while the trail of her magic encircled Shade's feet.

"I found him." Sound returned at her announcement. As did every other one of her senses. She inhaled his scent deeply and brushed a finger down the arm of one of Shade's shadowed figures.

"I was coming for you," Shade whispered as he met her gaze, adoration in his expression. Kora smiled at him.

Áxios moved in alongside her and stared at the immortal who held their brothers. "This last part is for both of you."

Without another word, all three siblings vanished. The door snapped shut with a resounding click and all that remained was she and Shade and a thousand unsaid words.

# CHAPTER 15

THEY STARED AT EACH OTHER. Neither moved. Kora called back the trail that had led her to the God of the Dead like an X that marked a spot.

Shade's mouth quirked. "We can leave whenever you want."

"Oh?" At the moment, leaving was the last of her concerns. She had no doubt that he was right, but while they were locked in a room together, Kora knew it was time to air out their grievances. If they walked out the front door, would all her insecurities and his secrets be left unsaid? Within Áxios' speech had been hints of what they still had to prove—to each other and the other gods. Kora knew this was their final challenge. She wouldn't disregard the gods' need for reassurance. For the sake of her world, she didn't blame them for their concern. Words were one thing. They had eternity to prove they meant them.

But she had no intention of leaving Shade alone. "Do you think we should leave?"

He played with the cuff of his coat. "No."

"Do you think the Triad is listening at the door?" It was a valid question, and she couldn't help but return Shade's grin.

"Not if they know what's good for them."

Storing up all the courage she had, she finally said the words that lingered with her all evening, "Why are you upset that I'm turning immortal?"

Shade slowly blinked twice, then stared in confusion. "What?"

"You were upset that I was no longer going to be human. Was the idea of forever with me so disappointing?" As soon as she said them aloud, she knew them to be untrue. But it felt good to get them off her chest.

He rushed across the room and enveloped her in a tight hug, pulling her close. "No," he whispered in her ear. "No. Never. A thousand times no."

Tears stung at the back of her eyes.

He pulled back and cupped her face in his hands. "I'm sorry if that's what you thought. The idea of an hour, a day, a millennium with you is nothing but a happy thought with a million possibilities."

"Then are you worried that I too will leave you alone?"

The shine of his eyes flickered for a moment. With a deep breath, he released the truth. "Every second of every day."

She inhaled sharply at the admission, her heart hurting for the immortal who had known nothing but abandonment.

"I don't ever want to leave you, and I never want to be without you, Kora. But I would accept that decision if it is one you choose. It would hurt, but I wouldn't blame you for it."

Her eyes dampened. "I don't want to leave you either, Shade. Never. Whenever we are apart, I do everything in my power to keep busy and distracted so I don't think only of you. I keep my window open in hopes you will visit. This last month without you has been torture."

"I'm so sorry." He kissed her forehead, his lips pressed to her skin for two beats before he pulled back and searched her eyes. "I love you."

Her heart stuttered in the best way possible. A few tears misted his lashes as Shade continued, "I regret not telling you sooner about the changes you are going through. Worse still, that you didn't receive my letters."

"You should have told me in person anyway. For something like this, letters would not have been appropriate."

His mouth fell into a frown. "You're right."

"I also wanted to talk to you about the invitation, but you didn't even seem to care that I was going to the masquerade. I wanted you here with me." All her emotions surfaced as though she was a kettle ready to scream.

His brow furrowed. "Astraea was the first to mention the masquerade to me. I am trying hard not to take over your life and let you make your own choices."

"So you're keeping me at an arm's length?"

Shade's mouth opened, then closed. His shoulders drooped. "Maybe I was. But that was never my intention. I was terrified I'd smother you, so I didn't even consider you'd want me to come tonight."

"Of course I did." It was time to bare all her insecurities. "And I doubted that you wanted to be with me when I heard you received an invitation."

Shade shook his head. "If you haven't noticed, Velos lives for drama. It is no excuse, but the reason I came tonight was to find you. If I'd received the invitation earlier, I would have intervened."

She reached out and brushed his copper hair from his brow. "I believe you."

"I'm glad to hear that. I have no intention of lying to you." He swallowed, resting his hands on her hips and tugging her closer. "I could never be upset that you and I could be together forever."

She wanted to kiss him then but stopped herself as he rested his forehead against hers. "What I am is upset with myself for not telling you just how much I care about you before your mortality was questioned. I was trying to give you time—to not pressure you or to come on too strong."

"Why?" She needed to hear him say it. "Why did you not want to tell me the truth about my power?"

"Because I wanted to tell you those words, the truth of

how I feel, and for you to know that it doesn't matter if it's a few weeks, months, or eternity—I would always love you."

She was definitely crying now, tears tracking down her cheeks. "I love you too."

He kissed her then, and she melted into him as his arms wrapped tightly around her. He scooped her up, his mouth still on hers as he carried her to the sofa in the center of the room. He pulled back long enough to look over her body. "It's you, Kora. It's always you. Being apart from you this past month has been torture for me too. I thought I could find all the answers and give you options. Are you going to be all right with all of this?"

"Yes." She sighed. "Now, kiss me." She dug her fingers into his arms, pulling him closer. "Prove to me that you're here."

He grinned as he leaned in, pressing a kiss to the corner of her mouth. His hand went up to the gold cord holding back her hair and gently removed it. With slow movements, he removed pins until her curls fell to her shoulders. Shade ran his fingers through her waves, his other hand wrapping around her waist to pull her even closer. "First, dance with me? I had to watch you dance with others tonight and only was given a moment of you within my arms."

"There isn't any music." She got to her feet as he pulled her up from the chair.

Shade pressed his body against hers and met her gaze. "We will find our own music. We always have."

She smiled back, and they began to move. A waltz. A simple box step of one to four as he led her around the room. And music appeared—in the whisper sounds of their steps, the beat of their hearts, and the swish of her dress as he spun her. Sound and sensation increased, and Shade dipped her again, her body arching towards the ground. As she slowly came upright, he worshipped the deep V of her dress, pressing lingering kisses to her as his lips trailed up her bare skin to her throat. She gripped his neck, pressing his mouth firmly against her neck, and dragged her fingers through his hair to grip his roots and turned his mouth to hers.

Shade groaned against her, tasting her. His tongue asked for entrance she could never deny.

He slowly backed her up until she was pressed against the small desk. He pulled her leg around his waist and drew her up until she was sitting on the edge. His fingers slid down to play with the straps of her shoes while he kissed her with a need and passion that went beyond anything she had ever felt before. "I love you," he whispered into her mouth.

His hand trailed up the slit of her dress, and goosebumps rose in the wake of his touch along her bare thigh. "I love you." He peppered each movement with the words, consumed by saying them as she was by hearing them.

She reached for his suspenders and tugged him between her legs to kiss him deeply. "I need you to show it now."

He chuckled. "You still don't believe me?"

"Oh, I do." She pulled both straps off his shoulder until they hung at his sides, before unbuttoning each of the buttons of his shirt with just as much deliberation as he had shown her. "But I need to feel you inside me."

He groaned at her words and he reached for her, but Kora pulled back to place a hand on his chest. She pushed gently, and a grin lifted at the corner of his mouth as he stepped back, one after another, until his legs touched the edge of the four posted bed on the far wall. As she was about to push him down, he wrapped his arms around her and consumed her mouth, kissing her with fierce need. He turned and laid her on the bed, bracing himself above her as he bent close. She continued her attempts to free every one of his buttons, revealing his toned bronze chest. The dip of his waist. Each of the abdominal muscles that she trailed her fingernails over. He hissed at her touch, his head buried at her throat, and her body arching into him in response to the sensation of the trail of his tongue.

When the last button was undone, he straightened and she immediately felt the loss of his body heat but watched with fervor as he tugged the shirt off and dropped it to the ground. He reached for the top button of his pants, but she sat up and grabbed hold of his wrists. "Let me."

He dropped his hands to his side as she took each button of his trousers and slipped them through the small hole until his trousers hung loose on his hips. She released him from his undershorts, wrapping her hand around his shaft and gave it one firm pump. He groaned out as she applied pressure and did it again.

"Kora—"

She smiled up at him, and his knees buckled as she gave him one more long pump. "Are you all right?"

"Yes," he breathed.

"Good." She pressed a kiss to the tip of him, then curled her mouth over the head.

"Shit—" He shuddered against her, gripping his hands in her hair and tugging her head back, her mouth releasing him with a pop. "If you aren't careful, I'll come much sooner than either of us would like."

"I'm trying to make you feel good."

He leaned down and kissed her deeply, his hand still tangled within her hair, and his other tugging aside the sleeve of her dress to reveal her breast.

Gentle fingers grazed along the peak of her nipple, knuckles kneading the dress off her other shoulder. With him distracted by each inch of her skin being revealed, her hand pumped him once more and his head knocked back.

Shade's movement became less calculated. He tugged her upwards, releasing the few buttons at the back of her dress near her behind and inched back as the dress pooled at her feet. He swallowed deeply, his throat bobbing as he looked her over in a way that made her feel just as loved as he claimed. Wanted in every sense of the word.

"You've always been beautiful, Wildflower. But you're also mine. From now until you don't want me anymore."

"From now until eternity," she corrected. "This isn't one-sided, Shade. I choose you." She pulled him closer as he stepped out of his trousers fully. "Let me show you just how much."

She initiated the kiss this time. Slow movements that counteracted his zealous desire. He shuddered as she grazed fingers over his bare skin. In the times they had shared a bed in the past six months, she'd never been the one to take control. But she'd learned a thing or two.

Kora turned him until the back of his knees were pressed against the bed. She pushed him back, then straddled his waist. He looked up at her, one hand on her hip, the other at her cheek before cupping her neck. "I love you, Shade." She looked into his eyes, making sure he knew it. "I don't ever want to leave you alone."

She wanted to brush away the tears from under his lashes, but the mask restricted movement. The God of the Dead was crying. She hadn't meant to bring him to tears, but she knew what those honest words meant to him.

"Eternity is a long time," he choked out.

"Then I'm glad mine will be with you."

She took the hand against her cheek and pressed a kiss to his palm, then took one of his fingers into her mouth, circling her tongue around the digit. He held her gaze as she shifted, until her entrance was centered over him and he guided his cock inside. She lowered herself slowly, watching his eyes shutter with each glorious inch of him she took, until he let out a moan that could have echoed the walls as she sat firmly on him. Deep. He was so deep. And her body reacted to that sensation. Her hips moved, gentle at first as she rocked back and forth with his finger in her mouth, then added a second. His free hand reached up and kneaded her breast. He pinched her nipple and her body shuddered. His mouth twisted into a mischievous grin, and he sat up to wrap an arm around her, releasing his fingers from her mouth.

"So deep," he groaned against her throat before kissing her, shifting his hips upwards as she pressed herself down on him. His mouth turned to her breasts, a nip at the sensitive skin. She lowered deeper into him, settling into this new position. Sweat clung to her skin as they moved together. His hand slid between them, playing with the bundle of nerves above their union. At the rising friction, their frantic movements, heat coursed through her. And the moment that his mouth tightened on her breast, she came undone.

As she cried out her release, he changed the movement just enough to keep it coming and her body shuddered against him as she slowly came down from the sensations coursing through her. She took his mouth with hers, rolled her hips against him, and forced his hand from between them as she pressed her fingers into his back. His arms dug into her thighs as she chased her pleasure. She leaned back, her body arching. Perspiration dripped down the curve of her breast, and he licked it with his warm tongue.

"I love seeing you this way." He grazed his finger over her throat, his thumb brushing her bottom lip, and she kissed the pad of skin. "Completely undone."

"You do this to me," she admitted.

He kissed her and she melted against him with her arms draped over his shoulders to bracket his back, his muscles taut from the strain to keep them upright.

He pulled back, and she rested her forehead against his. She closed her eyes, relishing in the feel of his body.

"Open your eyes and watch, Wildflower." He kissed her lips gently. "Watch and see what you do to me."

She did as he asked, the intensity of his gaze mesmerizing. They moved together. Their hips in a perfect synchronization for each other's pleasure that built up more and more. The friction of his body with hers. And as she came undone for the second time, their movements more frenzied, she held his gaze. And he broke apart. The room twisted with shadows as he came with a roar. He held her close as he began to shudder, his hands digging into her skin.

They found each other's mouths and kissed deeply. Her eyes pinched closed, tears sliding down her cheek, hoping he could feel every bit of the all-consuming love she had for him.

# CHAPTER 16

KORA WOKE ABRUPTLY. In her room. In her bed. Alone.

Had it not been for the dress hung on her wardrobe, she would have thought the previous night her own twisted dream. She flung aside her quilt, her underclothes on, and crossed the room to find a note folded over the shoulder of the dress with her name written in Shade's familiar script.

She opened the letter and smiled.

*Good morning, Wildflower,*

*I wish I could have stayed with you, but duties required my attention. I won't be gone from your side for long, though. A future needs to be finalized. Ours.*

*Sincerely,*

*Yours*

She drew a bath, and after she dressed quickly and ran a comb through her tangled hair. Part of her wanted to leave the knots alone as a reminder of what they had shared. The words they had spoken. But she was still confused as to how and when she had returned to her room. The last moment she remembered was Shade and her making love before curling up in his arms. His even breaths against her neck as he held her and she drifted off into sleep.

Magic. She smiled at her reflection in the mirror. Her body ached from the dancing, the lust—everything that entailed the previous night's activities. Yet, it was a good type of ache. One that she relished.

She hummed as she ate breakfast, barely aware of her mother's speculative glances. Her father was already at the office. Michael had asked how the night had gone, then sat down beside her as she grinned. "Good."

"That's all we are getting?" Mrs. Darling's brow rose. "You've looked as though you are walking on air. I haven't heard you ever hum at breakfast."

Kora finished her bite of rusk. She wondered if her mother remembered anything from the previous evening but wasn't daring enough to ask. "It was unlike anything I would have ever expected."

Mrs. Darling sipped her English tea primly, watching Kora who continued to eat as if famished. She had barely eaten more than the few hors d'oeuvres that had been passed around before the game officially started. Certainly not enough for the amount of energy she exuded. "Should I assume you met someone?"

Kora shrugged. "We shall see." She didn't want to say more about Shade, uncertain how much time would pass until his return. With him at the mansion all night, days had passed in Nekrós. They had been careful on his previous visits to keep them short. Since his stint as a collector of souls prior to reclaiming his title, he hadn't been gone from the Isles for such a long period of time. Hopefully, the time he'd spent on the Isles over the past few months had been enough to get everything back on track after his long absence.

After she had changed into her work clothes, she found her way to the flower beds and bean stalks to distract herself. Her gloved hands dug through the earth, and she cleared away the weeds, trying to pull them from the root. She looked at a plant with flowers blooming amongst the thistles, considering it before adding it to the pile by her leg. Bent over again, she heard Michael's clomping steps before he made his appearance known and cleared his throat. "What happened?"

She looked up at the sharpness of his tone to find him standing above her with arms crossed over his chest. "Who was he?"

Kora's brow rose. "Who was who?"

"This man that you obviously met last night. You couldn't have given up on Shade, could you?"

"Michael, please."

"No." He stomped his foot, appraising her. "He loves you. I know he hasn't said it—"

"Yes, he did. Last night."

Michael stopped short and stared. "He did? He was there?"

Kora blushed and nodded, sitting back on the heels of her boots. "He was."

"Oh?"

More questions flashed across his face but before any could come toppling from his mouth, Nanny called, "Kora. You have a visitor. Your mother has asked you to wash up and meet her in the drawing room."

She stood up, brushing her hands together to remove the excess dirt. With a quick glance over her shoulder, she ensured that Nanny was already back inside before she let her power flare to life. She took the weeds and relocated them to an empty flower bed. Michael watched wide eyed at the floating plants, and as the dirt moved aside by her power alone and the weeds were replanted.

He turned to her. "Why? They are just weeds."

"They are only weeds because they were amongst the plants I am trying to care for. They are still life, and just because I don't want them amongst my beans, doesn't mean they can't be helpful. Some of them attract bees and birds." She removed one glove at a time, then dusted off the knees of her gardening pants. Her mother wasn't aware of her state of underdress, but she didn't care. It was probably Ariana who came to call. She had hoped to see and to talk to her friend about her recollection of the previous evening. "Weeds are only a name for a collection. Not a description of what they offer the world."

Michael took her hand. "You know best. The flowers have always liked you." He glanced towards the door. "Nanny's watching now."

Kora had known the woman had returned, but she was confident that she hadn't seen a thing. "Our secret." A reminder.

"Yours and mine." He walked with her, hand in hand. "And Kora, I'm glad you're using your power more. You should."

She kissed the top of his head as they reached Nanny. The woman glanced out at the garden, then back at Kora. "You've been working hard."

"Yes."

"There is a gentleman to see you."

"What?" Kora's eyes widened. Could it be Shade? What was he thinking? Was he thinking?

Nanny smiled knowingly. "Did you listen to your head or your heart?"

"Both."

"Good." She bustled away, taking Michael with her.

Kora swallowed, her hands fidgeting with the hem of her shirt. She wasn't nervous about seeing who waited for her but was unprepared for what it could mean.

She was just about to enter the drawing room, then came to a stop when she heard voices from within.

"You and my daughter met last night?"

"We did."

The voice wasn't Shade's. She paled, quickly turning the corner and stopping in her tracks at the sight of Velos. "You."

He grinned, and Mrs. Darling got to her feet. "My dear, Mr. Vasilis came to call. Is there a problem?"

Kora wanted her mother out of the room immediately. "That depends on why he came here."

Velos bowed his head. "I understand. I will explain everything."

"There is no need." Shade had filled in the gaps for her the previous night.

"Kora, do we need to see him out? I can call for—"

"No. If we could have a moment though."

"I shouldn't leave—"

"Yes, Mother." Kora met her mother's worried gaze. "Please."

"It's not proper."

Velos sighed, and Kora turned her attention back to him just as her mother slowly exited, but her jilted movements said that she clearly didn't want to. "Let her go," Kora grumbled under her breath.

"I am just assisting her." Velos tilted his head. "He explained, I assume?"

Shade had told her everything while he held her in his arms before she fell asleep. "Yes. Which is why you don't need to be here or ever cross my path again."

"I understand your feelings. And after today, none of us will ever cross this threshold. But I cannot claim to believe our paths should never cross when eternity is at your door."

Her mouth tightened.

"I just came to offer an olive branch. One that maybe, over time, you will accept. We never meant ill will towards you or anyone in Athens."

"You think that makes it all right?" He shrugged and that only infuriated her more. "They are people. I'm a person. Even if things change" —she was careful how loud she spoke in case her mother was listening in— "that doesn't make what you did all right."

"We never took away anyone's choice. Our acolytes are loyal and wanted to be there. And in truth, we allow them to be who they want to be without question, suspicion, or doubt." He folded his hands behind his back. "None of them ever wanted to leave, or they would have left with your friend. They could be frivolous with their minds and their bodies. They could give into their wants and desires. That was not on me or my siblings. I didn't force them into beds or dark corners with one another. I just unlocked the opportunity for what could be. And they took it. For that, I cannot be held accountable."

"But your power—"

He shook his head. "Only enhances what is already there. As does Thélo's. They never needed saving."

Kora remembered their blank stares when Ariana left. How the Shade doppelgängers had been uncertain and confused. "You controlled their bodies—that is not all right. The gods shouldn't take away our will." She pinned him in her gaze, hoping that maybe he would see the error of his ways. "Even if you gave many of them an opportunity and a place to experience things they wanted, there is no excuse for the fact that you used them. You changed their appearances for a game. They weren't themselves when Áxios had me search for Shade. They were as much a pawn in your little trial as they were a distraction."

Velos' expression hardened. "You don't understand our world yet. You will someday. I hope you remember your little speech as time goes on. You already used one of our powers to change your parents' memory. Remember the lines you've drawn."

"I..." He was right, even if she knew it was for the best to erase her parents' memories from the night before, that didn't make it right. She would never be like them. That determination alone had her considering writing a journal to remind her of her humanity. "And me? Why couldn't I leave."

"Because of your curiosity."

She blinked. "What?"

"When the game wasn't active, you could have left at any time. But you needed the answers, didn't you?"

Kora wanted to deny it, but kept her mouth shut. She'd never even tried to leave except when her parents had appeared. The only time she had considered it was when Shade had been with her. Even leading up to the masquerade, she had only wanted the answers to who their host was and why she was the guest of honor.

She lifted her head, squaring up to him. "Yes."

"And do you despise the answers you received?"

She and Shade had learned more about each other. At the most, they learned how to communicate better. At the very least, they finally admitted how they felt. Kora swallowed. "No."

Velos nodded. "Good." He gave her a small bow. "It was a pleasure to meet you, Kora."

Then he was gone, disappearing in a blink.

Kora realized she was breathing heavily and closed her eyes to calm her anger and nerves.

Mrs. Darling appeared a few breaths later. "Where did he go?"

"He left."

"But I was in the hallway. I didn't see him—"

Her father came in with his jacket still on and briefcase in his hand. "Uh, sorry to interrupt."

Mrs. Darling whirled around. "There is something strange happening. There is—"

"Can this wait, my dear? There is someone here to visit our daughter."

Before Mother could continue, Mr. Darling moved aside to reveal Shade. Kora took a sharp breath at the sight of him in polished shoes, crisp trousers, and a clean cream-colored button up under a gray suit coat. He smiled at her with complete assurance. "Hello, Kora Darling."

It echoed a memory from what felt like a lifetime ago. When they first officially met on an isle meant for the dead. He'd been handsome then in his torn trousers, bare feet, and unkept hair. He looked older now, even though she knew that wasn't the case. "Hello."

"Mr. Galanis has come to call on our daughter."

Shade gave a small bow as a greeting to her mother. "It's a pleasure to meet you, Mrs. Darling."

"Shade?" Michael appeared, running straight to him and grabbing the immortal around the waist, squeezing him in a tight hug.

"Shade?" Mr. Darling's brow rose.

Michael paused his hug and turned to face their parents. "A nickname," he said with wide eyes. "It's what I call him."

"You know this man too, Michael?"

Kora bit her lip. "Yes, we originally met at the market."

"Yes. I was buying pomegranates." Shade winced slightly as Michael pulled on his arm.

"And then again last night," Kora added. The perfect reason as to why Shade made an appearance now, not before.

"Last night?" Mrs. Darling perked up, Velos' visit forgotten. "I see."

"I've come to ask if Miss Darling was available to show me her garden. She'd asked me to come by and see it."

"I can join them!" Michael declared. "I'll be their chaperone."

Kora pinched the bridge of her nose. "That's not necessary."

"It is," Mr. Darling agreed. "Stay with them." He turned to Kora. "Stay in the yard."

Kora hid her smile. Her father was back to his old self. Mr. Darling moved aside to allow Kora to pass but before she could, Shade turned towards him. "I hope upon our return, you and I could also speak and get to know one another."

Mr. Darling's brow rose. He cleared his throat, his gaze going between Kora and him. "I, well—yes, that will do."

"Thank you." Shade lifted the crook of his arm so Kora could wrap hers around his elbow, then walked out the door together with Michael following along at a skip. She was aware of her parents watching them carefully from a window as she stepped into the garden with Shade and Michael on his other side. He listened as she talked about one row of plants after the other. Michael interrupted from time to time, and Kora desperately wished he would find something to entertain himself with for just a moment so she could question Shade's appearance.

Michael finally seemed to catch her eye and started to skip ahead. "I'm going to look for bugs." He moved a few rows away and crouched down to search through the dirt.

Kora didn't know where to start. "Did you speak to Astraea?"

"This is your first question?" Shade grinned. "Yes. It was a long discussion where she told me that she didn't mind sharing our love letters but would not be involved in drama. So, instead, she caused it by not delivering my letter. She knew it contained information about your impending immortality and did not agree with telling you by missive."

Kora couldn't help but smile at the pixie's decision. "Well, I suppose we need to respect her wishes."

"It seems we do. Although, I see now that she had been right."

He turned to face her, and something about standing this close to him while her family lingered had her blushing.

"You're here," she whispered while watching Michael from the corner of her eye, unable to believe that Shade stood in her backyard.

"I'm here. I hope that's all right?"

"It's more than all right. But what does this mean?"

"A future."

She itched to touch him. "And what are you proposing?" Immediately her cheeks flushed from the insinuation. "Not that I'm trying to force—"

"Kora." He grinned at her. "If I could, I'd walk in there right now and ask your father for your hand. I want to do this right for you. For them too. They shouldn't worry about you."

She nodded. "I'd appreciate that."

"And I'm not coming here to take over your life. You still have aspirations. Ones that I do not want to interfere with. Here is what I want to offer, but please let me know what adjustments need to be made."

Kora took the hand he held out to her. He squeezed and then wrapped his other hand around hers. "I will procure a house here and in England."

She inhaled deeply.

"They will be ours. Yours and mine. You can continue your studies at whichever university you choose. I will not interfere in any way in what path is right for you. I will spend my time split between my responsibilities and being where you need and want me to be. I am at your beck and call. Then, at times, you will join me on my business ventures." She knew what all his words meant. He was tied to the Isles, and she still had to visit Nekrós monthly. "We will split our lives between the two. You have the independence you always craved, the opportunities you desire, and—"

"And you," she finished for him.

"And I will have you."

She nodded. His dream—his version of the future—was everything she had always hoped for. Freedom. A life. Only made better by him being in it. "I have only one amendment."

He kissed her knuckles, his eyes holding hers. "Anything."

"It's not just once a month I return with you, but whenever I please."

He rubbed his fingers over hers. "You want that?"

"I want you, Shade. All of you."

"You have all of me."

Kora stood on her tiptoes and kissed him. She was aware of her parents but didn't care. Not when his eyes widened, and he kissed her back, his fingers brushing her cheek. "Thank you," she breathed.

"For what."

She lowered again. "For understanding I still need to live."

"IT SEEMS OUR DAUGHTER IS ATTACHED." Mrs. Darling smiled from her place at the window. Her husband ran a hand over his face and fidgeted with his mustache. She knew he wished to interrupt Kora's stroll after the kiss, but she hadn't allowed it.

He sighed and removed something from his pocket. "Do you think she will still want this?"

Mrs. Darling took the envelope he held out towards her. Her eyes widened at Kora's name written in elegant script on the same page as Cambridge University stamp. She glanced at her daughter who stood beaming beside the man she undoubtedly loved as she watched her brother. Her attention shifted to Mr. Galanis who watched Kora with unquestionable affection.

"Yes." She smiled. "She will. And I think that gentleman will follow her anywhere."


***THE END***

# ACKNOWLEDGMENTS

As always, there are so many people to consider when it comes to writing a novella. Especially those who deserve all the appreciation.

Thank you to S.T. Fernandez for considering my writing worthy enough to be included in this venture. I've been so lucky to have met you, and I'm thankful that Smitten had a chance for us to meet and connect! You've become more than a writing friend.

To E.V Sauvage for the beautiful covers. I know taking on this process was a labor of love and I appreciate the time you took to work on them for our collaboration.

For Megan, the editor extraordinaire. Every time I call upon you, you're there! Thank you for the time you put into making my ramblings make sense.

Ashley...where do I begin but as always, I'm thankful for our check ins, our writing meetings, and the fact you always talk me off of the cliff where I would love to throw my laptop over.

Finally, to my family who is supportive even when they don't exactly know what I'm talking about. I love you and that you love me for me.

# BIBLIOGRAPHY

GW Prouse loves to write emotionally wounded characters healing (and finding love) in magical worlds. She has a heart for travel and a love of the outdoors that inspires her settings and worlds. If she's not writing or rushing her family around to the countless activities children can accumulate, she can be found crafting, or cuddling up with her gamer husband while she reads.

To Follow GW Prouse on social media or to learn more go to https://linktr.ee/GWProuse or scan the QR code.